For Cynt
Enjoy
J. Anthony Gallo

MW00965727

SAVED BY GLORY

J. ANTHONY GALLO

AZZURRO PUBLISHING

Saved By Glory

ISBN: 978-0-692-01734-0

Remembering The Man and The Woman

Larry and Ann

ACKNOWLEDGEMENTS

My many thanks to the following individuals that were instrumental in helping this book project to completion:

Ron, Marj, Karen, Kari, Marcus, Pat, Tricia, Jacquie

Illustrations for this book were done by Jacquie Gallo, Signature Member of the Colorado Watercolor Society.

FOREWORD

"Saved by Glory" is a tale of "good versus evil." It is a work of fiction based on a real-life (and death) experience of real people. The story revolves around the struggle between demons and angels for the soul of one Man. The central characters in the book are demons (fallen angels) and guardian angels. The people (the Man, the Woman, the Cousin, the Friend), while essential players, are unnamed.

The battle between good and evil started before time, before recorded history, and it will continue until the Day of Judgment shall come. The story is set in 1993, not that long ago in the history of men and women, but well before the advent of portable computing and social media that offer instantaneous personal contact around the globe. Still, even as innovation progresses, little changes in the ongoing battle between heaven and hell.

Revelation. Ch. 12: 7-17

And there was war in heaven: Michael and his angels fought with the Dragon; and the Dragon and his angels fought, but they did not prevail, nor was a place found for them in heaven any longer. And the great Dragon was cast out, that serpent of old, called the Devil and Satan, who deceives the whole world. He was cast out into the earth, and his angels were cast out with him. Then I heard a loud voice saying in heaven, "Now salvation, and strength, and the kingdom of our God, and the power of His Christ have come, for the accuser of our brethren, who accused them before our God day and night, has been cast down. And they overcame him by the blood of the Lamb and by the word of their testimony, and they loved not their lives unto the death. Therefore rejoice, O heavens, and you who dwell in them! Woe to the inhabitants of the earth and the sea! For the devil has come down to you, having great wrath, because he knows that he has a short time."

Now when the Dragon saw that he had been cast to the earth, he persecuted the woman who gave birth to the male Child. But the woman was given two wings of a great eagle, that she might fly into the wilderness to her place, where she is nourished for a time and times and half a time, from the presence of the serpent. So the serpent spewed water out of his mouth like a flood after the woman, that he might cause her to be carried away by the flood. But the earth helped the woman, and the earth opened its mouth and swallowed up the flood which the Dragon had spewed out of his mouth. And the Dragon was enraged with the woman, and he went to make war with the rest of her offspring, who keep the commandments of God and have the testimony of Jesus Christ.

I

THE TIME: *O'dark thirty, August, 1993.*

THE PLACE: *Tartarus*

"I have a prospect."

"Where?"

"Memphis."

"Tell me about it. Man or woman?"

Moloch hesitated. This was going to be complicated, and he wanted to be sure he explained it clearly the first time. Lucifer, a.k.a. Satan, Beelzebub, Baalzebul, the Tempter, The Dragon, had been a little temperamental lately. In fact, he was very much acting like, "The Dragon." And Tartarus beware if any demon called him other than "Lucifer."

"I was Lucifer when we came to Tartarus, I will be Lucifer when we leave." Moloch had heard that many times. The other names were given by men influenced by

Jehovah God. Jehovah God knew Lucifer felt diminished by such names.

Tartarus was home to the fallen angels and their leader. Moloch was a fallen angel—now an ancient demon. Having a vainglorious estimate of his shining appearance, Moloch's pride was his downfall. He joined Lucifer, the Devil, and was in the forefront of the ancient battle against Michael. Now banished to lower earth, Moloch was old, bent, wrinkled and a decayed green color. Moloch hated green! But he had come to love his forked tail—even if it were green too. The barbs on the end were fine for lashing both recalcitrant goblins and uppity witches. He liked to threaten and torture lost souls with it too.

Moloch was more accomplished than most of the demons and, lately, witches who came to Tartarus. His seniority and his prowess for evil assured his almost immediate access to the Satan whenever he requested it. Moloch was careful not to abuse that privilege. Lucifer on whim would get tired of his attendants and courtiers and banish them for a century or two to Gehenna.

Moloch had no dislike of Gehenna, or Hell or Hades as men called it, but he did enjoy the freedom of movement between Tartarus, Gehenna and the garbage spots on earth. Sheol was a different matter. Sheol was the equivalent of utter destruction for men. It was the place of total darkness, complete forgetfulness and absolute silence. No thought or whisper of earth, Gehenna or Tartarus existed there. Even demons were uncomfortable in Sheol, and Moloch was no exception.

Yes, Tartarus beware the Satan's fouler mood in this epoch. Whereas before Lucifer had enjoyed a good challenge--the more devious and evil the better--recent reverses had made him more short-tempered. The world of men was doing better. The brutality of the Soviet system was disappearing; the four horsemen were on the run in the Middle East despite recent gains in Somalia; and, there was a possibility men would recover reason and try to overturn Baba's mischief in the area that used to be Yugoslavia. There was even a rumor from Ahriman that the Pope might meddle in the Yugoslav situation. Moloch wished he could remember what all those little areas of men's pride were called, but the former Yugoslavia was Baba's concern and he, Moloch, really had other plans to worry about.

Moloch was after a soul. He had been working on this particular prospect, the Man, for a long time. There was one complicating factor—the Woman. The Woman was strong and her influence on the Man was strong also. That's why Moloch had confidence in his current plan.

Tap, tap...tap, tap. Moloch realized that Lucifer was tapping his cloven, left foot awaiting an answer. He had been daydreaming trying to sort out the best way to explain the plan.

"Master, the subject is a woman, but the prospect is a man."

"Why not both?"

"Master, the Woman is too strong. She is true to Jehovah God and has a deep Christian faith. I was sure the

Man was ours until he met the Woman. Her goodness envelopes him like Jacob's coat. She...."

"What!" There was an ominous rumble in the sulfurous air. Lucifer, now truly The Dragon, leaned forward, eyes glinting, mood darkening.

Damn. There it was again. Moloch felt he was bewitched. One of those angels had somehow bewitched him. He was always doing battle with guardian angels for men's souls. Somewhere, somehow one of them had bewitched him into using Biblical references. The problem was that Moloch liked Biblical references. Lucifer didn't.

And it was wrong! "Joseph…Joseph's!!!….It was Joseph's Coat!" Moloch almost screamed.

Oh no! Too late! It was "Joseph's coat." Moloch covered his error—his anguish—with a muffled cough. Lucifer—uncharacteristically—missed it. Otherwise Moloch would have felt a jolt of searing, burning, brimstone fire before being banished.

Moloch took a breath and keened, "Sorry Master, I mean that the Man was a true rascal until he met the Woman. He was wild. He cared for little. He believed that intelligence of mind was the only true value of life. But after meeting the Woman he started to change and he allowed her goodness to influence him. Her grace with God was so strong that even her own guardian angel could help protect the Man."

Lucifer continued the hard stare, but Moloch noticed he did relax a bit.

MOLOCH-
GRADUATION PHOTO

II

"We thought we would get the Man back several years ago. We had a good chance. He and the Woman lived in Okinawa--Naha Air Base. The Man was a military pilot. They were far from home and their relatives; in those days the mail was slow. Overseas telephone, particularly in the Pacific, was almost impossible. The Man's twin brother, to whom he was very close, suddenly became ill and died even before the Man heard of his illness. The Man not only felt a deep personal loss, but he felt a physical vulnerability that was new to him."

"This was the time of the so-called Cuban Missile Crisis when you, oh Lord Satan, almost had your third world war in one century." A little flattery wouldn't hurt here thought Moloch, but not to overdo it as the ultimate failure of Satan's forces to spark a nuclear war was not to be dwelt upon.

"The Man's squadron was standing alert, and he could not go back to the United States to see his bereaved family and attend the funeral. With the squadron on alert the Man still had to fly, sometimes flying to and remaining at other bases, leaving his wife home alone in a strange country at a dangerous time. For the first time he was uneasy in his own mortality. The pressures from his personal crisis and the fear for his family in the world crisis became great, and the Man retreated into religion of the mind. The Woman's faith became stronger, but the Man retreated further from God. He dabbled in New Age religions and religions of the East. He was truly lost.

"As I said, the Man was a pilot--a jet fighter pilot--and we planned some mischief on one of his flights. We were certain that in his confused and spiritually weakened condition, his soul could be easily won. It was monsoon season on Okinawa, and the weather was naturally bad. The clouds were solid from 500 feet to 45,000 feet—an unwelcome opportunity for dangerous vertigo. We made the weather a lot worse by hiding thunderstorms in the clouds."

"The airplane the pilot was on the schedule to fly was in bad repair due to extra effort by gremlins we recruited. The aircraft mechanics were doing good work finding, repairing and logging the gremlins' mischief in the aircraft maintenance forms, but we countered by inducing paperwork errors. That which appeared to be fixed really wasn't. Actually, the airplane was unfit to fly--and, the ejection seat would not work. We disabled the pin that would fire the explosive charge. Our plan was that the plane would crash and we would steal another soul for you, Master."

"What happened?"

Had to be careful here thought Moloch. It was hard not to lie as that was the very core of his nature. No lying, he thought. That would only make matters worse. Keeping the story short and simple was the best way to deflect further wrath. He already was in trouble with that stupid reference to Jacob's coat.

"Well Master, we, Asmodeus and I, had expected the pilot's assigned airplane to carry only one pilot as most of them did. Unfortunately, at the last minute the maintenance supervisor grounded the scheduled airplane. It was due for what he called a "100 hour inspection." The replacement airplane that day was a two-seater--it carried two pilots."

It was always dangerous to mention lost battles. Maybe the reference to Asmodeus would help. He was senior to Moloch in Satan's hierarchy and one of Lucifer's favorites,

"So?"

"It's true the Man was a fighter pilot and fighter pilots could be a pretty rowdy, rutty, lot--particularly in those days. But somehow more Christians were showing up as fighter pilots. Or, maybe more fighter pilots were showing up as Christians. Probably had something to do with that stupid poem, 'Highflight'."

"Harrumph!" from Lucifer. Sitting on his black throne with attendants now carefully increasing their distance from him, the normally generous space seemed to get smaller. The Dragon was an ominous presence with all the indications of impatient anger. The throne room seemed to darken. Sulfurous fumes thickened and boiled across the dark ceiling.

I did it again thought Moloch. Moloch knew he had to abandon his tendency to explain everything and detour on discourse or he would never get through this interview without some serious, brimstone burns. If he could only keep it short and simple, he would prevail and get extra help from Lucifer in stealing that soul.

"Master, the other pilot had a guardian angel."

"What?" The malevolence was growing. The always present mood of evil was intensifying. "You didn't know?" growled The Dragon. His color was deepening. The witches in attendance were completely gone from the room now. The other demons moved back to the walls by the doors. The ogres remained where they were, but ogres were seldom smart enough to sense danger.

"We had planned very carefully. We worked for weeks on the weather. Asmodeus was particularly clever in influencing the airplane mechanics and initially directing our gremlins. We insured the airplane records were all messed up. Unfortunately, our recruited gremlins got out of control and they couldn't resist playing more with this one airplane instead of breaking another as we had told them to do. The airplane was literally falling apart on the parking ramp. The deterioration was too obvious and the maintenance line chief decided to double-check the airplane records. He was too good, and our gremlins had been too messy. The airplane records were a disaster. The line chief grounded that airplane for an inspection as I said. Consequently, our intended victim had to fly in the replacement airplane with the extra pilot."

Moloch and Asmodeus had harsh words over the airplane mix-up. There was still a little hard feeling. Up to that time, Asmodeus had stolen eight straight souls without a fight. He was not pleased with the surprises and failure after months of work.

"And the extra guardian angel?" Lucifer asked quietly. His soft tone made Moloch even more uneasy.

"Franciscus, Master. His name was Franciscus. We did try sickness on the new pilot at the last minute, but it didn't work. Franciscus managed to intervene. The pilot became sick only after the flight was over. There just wasn't enough time. We tried some last minute weather changes. We strengthened the thunderstorms buried in the thick clouds and managed extra lightning. We even caused some ground navigation equipment to short out by breaching a roof in the heavy rain. The planned crash did not occur. The other pilot's guardian angel, Franciscus, was very skillful, and very powerful. And we hadn't expected Cornelius to show up when we were trying to wreck the jet fighter.

"As I mentioned, Cornelius is the Woman's guardian angel, but we learned too late that her grace with God is so great that Cornelius sometimes helped the Man. We engaged in forty-five minutes of ploy and counter ploy. We were dealing with two guardian angels. Franciscus and Cornelius seemed to know what we were going to do before we did it. We could not make the plane crash. We did achieve a flameout on the engine, but the second pilot's skill was great. His guardian fortified that pilot's reserve, and our efforts to create panic with a lightning strike were ignored. In fact, he laughed, Master. The other pilot laughed!"

The memory of that laughter heightened Moloch's disappointment. It was a memory he could not shake and he was afraid it would be with him through eternity. It heightened his natural dislike of guardian angels--and fighter pilots.

Moloch continued, "With the help of the guardian angels, the other pilot and the Man worked as a team and landed safely. The Man escaped our carefully laid plans. We have had no good opportunity to steal his soul since."

Moloch had been so upset and so exhausted by the struggle with the two guardian angels that he had retired to Tartarus for a long rest. It had been years since he again saw Asmodeus, the other defeated demon.

Quickly he resumed his account to Lucifer, "But now the Man may again be weak, and we have a chance."

"A chance or an opportunity?" from the Tempter.

"Oh, an opportunity, Master. A great opportunity! The Woman has been sick. She was sick with the same disease before but recovered. Now the disease has returned, and we believe that God will call her home. Ahriman, who I consulted because he is smarter in these things than I, thinks it is part of the Plan. If so, the Man would be very vulnerable. The theft of his soul would be so easy."

Moloch would never understand "The Plan", but that did not mean he wouldn't take advantage whenever possible. He preferred to fight with devious measures; the more evil the better, but the direct, simple approach also had merits. A soul was a soul, and he would steal any soul for his master, Lucifer, any way he could. Let Lucifer worry about the Plan and the strange rules they had to follow in their war with Jehovah God.

Jehovah God had a Plan in creating the earth and the heavens. As Creator, Jehovah God was the law. Lucifer had become jealous of both God and the men made in God's image. Lucifer wanted to destroy mankind in his fight with God and thus vanquish God himself. But for now, Lucifer had to follow the rules of The Plan Jehovah God used in creating heaven and earth. Lucifer believed if he could create chaos, he could break the rules, he could then destroy The Plan ruled by Jehovah God. For Lucifer, The Satan, stealing men's souls was the best road to chaos and ultimate victory. It was his intent that the fallen angels, his demons, scourge all mankind with evil, murder, pestilence, famine and war to weaken even the strongest. The demons would do anything to steal souls. Lucifer was convinced that he could regain heaven if he stole enough souls. He was merciless to demons who failed.

"The Man remains an atheist?" asked Lucifer. "The Woman has not won him over for God? He remains, I believe in your words, rowdy and rutty?"

"No, Master. Not an atheist, the Man is an agnostic. He does lead a benevolent life, but his religion is superficial. It is intellectualism. He will not understand when God calls the Woman home. More so, he will not accept it. I know we can steal his soul. It may take some work but overall, we are confident of easy success."

"We?"

"Master, Asmodeus and I had agreed to again collaborate on this when the opportunity arose. The Man has remained on our minds since we lost the battle over him last time."

Lucifer was interested. As Moloch had said, a soul was a soul, and production had fallen off lately. "What about Christian friends and family? You did mention the Woman had a guardian angel didn't you?"

"Cornelius is the guardian angel. He is very clever, Master." Angels were supposed to be good, not clever, but clever was the highest accolade Moloch could think of. "There are some Christian friends, but the Man and Woman just moved to Memphis. You know how standoffish modern man is; they won't have had time to make new friends. The Woman's mother is very ill, and we are sure God will call the mother home very soon. We feel certain we can take advantage. The Woman's extended family is Christian with a strong faith, but they are not close to the Man who is our target. I am confident, but I do need the assistance of Asmodeus."

"Done," said Lucifer, his red skin darkening as he spoke. "No more of those silly, flimsy excuses. You mew like a human. I demand results, Moloch. I want that soul. Is that a problem? Sheol awaits those who fail. This time, no outcome other than complete success will be tolerated."

Moloch suddenly realized that today, he truly was dealing with "The Dragon." It was no small threat. The Satan was taking a personal interest in this. Trying to appear completely confident, he still could only muster a weak reply, "Yes, Master, no problem."

GROUNDED : GREMLINS

III

Moloch arranged to meet with Asmodeus and discuss the new plan to steal the Man's soul. Asmodeus had been out of touch so Moloch wanted to make sure the current situation and details were clear to his demon ally. Lucifer had strongly emphasized they could not afford to lose another battle for the Man's soul. There could be no surprises--at least, no major surprises. They met over the Golden Gate Bridge. The meeting place was a concession to Asmodeus who had been vacationing in Somalia soaking up the despair, grief and evil. Asmodeus liked the smell of big cities, San Francisco in particular, and the ghosts from Alcatraz were comforting also.

"Jacob's coat?" smirked Asmodeus.

Moloch ignored the jibe. "You are doing well?" he asked.

"Yes," replied Asmodeus. "Somalia was fun, but it was awfully crowded with demons. To what mischief do I owe this call?"

"Do you remember the Man when we battled Cornelius and Franciscus? I am going to steal the Man's soul. Conditions are favorable, but I am sure that Cornelius will interfere once again and your help will be needed. The Man and the Woman moved from San Francisco to Memphis to be near her mother who is gravely ill. The Woman is also now very sick and is in the Memphis Regional Hospital. She has had a reoccurrence of a serious illness. Ahriman thinks God will call her home soon. Maybe we can hurry her departure with some mischief. The Man is an agnostic. His faith is in himself and the Woman. He has moved away from allowing her grace with God and faith to extend to him. The Man is still a pilot and is often gone from the Woman, increasing his burden. The Man will not accept her being called home. He will be very angry and lost. We will then steal his soul."

"But, you do expect trouble from Cornelius?"

"Yes, but not too much. I see him working in isolation. Without the Woman's presence he won't be much help to the Man. He cannot stay with the Man. The Man does not have God's grace for a guardian angel."

"OK. I will meet you at the Memphis Regional Hospital tomorrow. It will be interesting to see the Man again. We can laugh at Cornelius while we steal the Man's soul." Moloch smiled at the thought, but still he was worried about the warning from The Satan.

Moloch was at the hospital at sunup. It was always best to be established before the hospital chaplain made his rounds. Something was wrong. He could feel the power of prayer. It hurt. Had he under-estimated the chaplain? No, it's the Woman. Damn, damn, damn he thought. Prayer around the hospital was natural, but the aura around the Woman's room was much stronger than he expected.

"Hello, Moloch." It was Cornelius and another guardian angel. "You are wasting your time here. But if you wish, you could enlighten us about the 'coat.'" Both were smiling at him.

Moloch didn't like that and glared back. No response was his best tactic. Who was the other guardian angel? He looked more carefully into the hospital room where the Woman lay. Moloch's understanding of the equipment monitoring the Woman was very good. She obviously had taken a turn for the worse. Good. The sooner she was gone, the sooner Cornelius was gone, and the sooner he would get the Man. Ah, a Friend of the Woman was there by the bed. That explained the other guardian angel, Mercy 1021 he learned. Without commenting, Moloch perched on the window sill. A little observation was in order. Let them waste their time thinking he was after the Woman's soul. When it was too late, the Man's soul would be his prize.

Sitting there on the window sill, Moloch was almost preening in early self congratulations. The blinding flash of light knocked him across the room. "Job's nose!" he cried. What had happened? The sun should never come in this room. He looked out the window and then ducked. A reflection off the building across the street was streaming in the window. Moloch winced, and then noticed Cornelius laughing by the door. The reflected sunlight had disappeared, and the other guardian joined Cornelius. Until now Moloch had never seen sunlight "bend" around a building. He had heard other demons tell of angels reflecting sunlight to direct it, but he had never believed the stories. The smiles of the two guardian angels and the burn across his shoulders required Moloch to reassess the truth of those stories.

"Go away, Moloch," advised Cornelius. "I know why you are here. Just as you were defeated before, you will be defeated again. There are no souls for you here."

It was hard for angels to look menacing, but both Cornelius and Mercy 1021 were very good at it. Moloch did not reply, but blended into the far corner.

Moloch spent the next few days waiting. His position in the corner was cramped, but he was determined to be patient for the short time it would take. It was obvious the Woman would be gone soon. The Friend visited daily and Mercy 1021, her guardian angel, continued to make Moloch uncomfortable. The Man also visited daily. Moloch was careful not to let either guardian angel see his interest in the Man even if they did know his plan.

"Ack!" Not again. He was faint. He looked to see if somehow sunlight had been directed upon him again, but all was quiet.

"What is this?" losing control, he cried. There was a third guardian angel in the room. The Cousin! He had forgotten the Cousin. Naturally she had a guardian angel. Her Cristobal was a strong angel. Moloch fled cursing.

Where was Asmodeus? He couldn't handle three angels. Most demons couldn't handle even two. He had been prepared for Cornelius. He had expected the Cousin and her guardian, but the Friend and her guardian had confused him. Also, the aura of prayer had subtly increased each day. There were more meddling Christians in this affair than he had counted on. He noticed prayer aura even around the Man. Asmodeus was not going to be happy. But then, where was Asmodeus?

"Memphis, Tennessee, you piece of sandstone!" complained an outraged Asmodeus. "I have been in every hospital in Memphis, Tennessee. I, naturally, did not find the Woman. Thinking she was gone as Ahriman predicted, I visited every Air Force, Navy and Marine air base in Tennessee looking for the Man. I have been on some wild airplane rides trying to find him. Despite being good prospects, fighter pilots are not my favorite people. They are too unpredictable. I finally found Ahriman and asked him where you were.

"So it was the Memphis in Texas, not Tennessee--a small detail that you omitted. And the Man is no longer a fighter pilot, but an airline pilot. Anything else I need to know?"

Asmodeus was fuming. Moloch could feel the heat. It made him smile which made it all so much worse. Asmodeus was gone in a flash.

"Just as well," thought Moloch. "It will be better if Asmodeus has time to settle down before I tell him about the extra guardian angels and the prayer auras."

IV

The Woman's earthly body died the next day and her soul was called home to be with Jehovah God. Through Cornelius she was aware of Moloch and knew the Man was the game. Cornelius, with his concern over the Woman, had not seen it initially, but the other guardians made it clear and he saw the logic of it. He made the Woman aware as together they approached Jehovah God.

"Welcome home, and well done my good and faithful servant."

Kneeling before God's love, the Woman and Cornelius made known their plea. "The Man," said the Woman. "The Man is in danger and must be saved. You must save him."

Cornelius added, "Moloch is there. He is intent upon the Man. He tried to steal the Man's soul before, but lost after a hard struggle."

"I know," said God, "but the Man has not followed the Word. By my grace he was saved before, but he does not believe. If he does not believe, he cannot be saved."

"But he is a good man," said the Woman. "He is a generous man, a kind man."

"You know the Word, Cornelius," responded God. But his answer was to the Woman as well.

"The power of prayer, Lord?" asked Cornelius.

"I know. I have heard the prayers. Many Christians love him. I have seen the aura of others' prayers surrounding him. He may be a good man. OK, see what you can do."

Disconsolate at the death, the Man had returned home alone. Moloch was hovering nearby and gleeful at the absence of guardian angels, he burned out a light bulb to further bother the Man. He whispered words to the Man, words of anger...abandonment...failure.... This was going to be easy, Moloch just knew it. Asmodeus was nowhere around, but Moloch needed no help. This soul was his to take alone.

The Man was staring out the window at the lake beyond. He was sitting in the family room at the back of the apartment. The room had French doors with windows on either side giving a wide view to the lake scene. The small lake was surrounded by golf course greenery. The sky was clear with only a few high clouds trying to interrupt a setting, yellow sun.

Moloch darkened the lake waters. He stilled the wind. He slipped the radio station down the band to play dreary music that was terrible for the Man--and perfectly delightful for Moloch. The Man was calling the Woman.

Moloch grinned. There would be no answer. In a matter of time, a short time, the Man would be his prize.

"I loved you--a sign--something--I do want to believe."

The Woman heard and looked at Cornelius. He nodded. "Let's go look," he said.

The Woman recoiled at the site of Moloch. An ugly, bent little manlike being with overlong arms, no ears, something that maybe was a nose between pinpoint, black eyes and teeth like a shark. Cornelius reached out and steadied her.

"Pay him no mind. He is harmless to one in a state of grace," advised the guardian. "Begone Moloch; there is nothing for you here."

Moloch flashed a toothy smile at the Woman. "I will win my prize," he said. In an effort to prove his point he caused another light to go out. The Man did not notice the change in light but remained staring out the window.

Cornelius advised the Woman, "Go by the chair. The Man may feel the presence of your spirit. I have an errand. Do not be bothered by the funny, little ogre. He can do nothing." He then whispered, "Keep the Man in the chair. Your presence will be sufficient to do that. Ignore the ogre."

Cornelius' words made Moloch angry, but they were true, except of course the part about being an ogre. Cornelius knew full well Moloch was once an angel, albeit a "fallen angel" and now a demon. Demons had status; ogres did not. The slight was intended.

Moloch could do nothing but wait. Waiting didn't bother him if there were a prize to be gained. He thought about following Cornelius. No, there was nothing Cornelius could do. The presence of the Woman's spirit would not be strong to the Man as long as Moloch and his own evil aura remained near.

"George 6234, I need help," said Cornelius.

George 6234 settled down next to Cornelius. If it were Cornelius, it would be fun. He and George had had some real battles with demons. George 6234 liked Cornelius' style. Pitched battles were fun, but Cornelius also liked to finesse the demons into defeat. Recovering from a brimstone burn, the result of a recent force of demons and ogres arrayed over one of men's bloody riots, George 6234 thought he was ready for finesse.

"We have to hurry." Cornelius provided a background briefing. "A sign is needed. I know just the thing, but we will need the sun."

Cornelius immediately had seen the solution upon seeing the Man and his environs. It was one he had used before. With George 6234 and the Woman this one would be easy despite Moloch. In fact, he was sure it was going to surprise the little demon. The Woman's presence would keep Moloch distracted--he hoped.

Cornelius surveyed the scene. He wanted to make sure his initial evaluation of the layout was correct. The Man, the chair, the bush, the sun, and the building across the lake were aligned just as he had remembered. "George 6234 ," he called, "I need a spot of dew."

"Dew?"

"Yes. Put it in the bush, in this fork of branches, right here."

George 6234 went to the lake and scooped up some water in the palm of his hand. He blew on it and molded it to fit the spot in the bush pointed out by Cornelius. It was slippery, but he held it in place until the surface tension of the new dew drop adapted to the branch's fork and the rough bark. It started to slip, but he blew on it gently and the dew drop stayed put.

Cornelius, staying out of sight so as to not disturb Moloch, peered around the corner of the porch. The Man remained in the chair idly staring out the window. The Woman's spirit remained by his side, her hands on his shoulders. Moloch was dancing around trying to drive the Woman off. Just as Cornelius had advised, she ignored the demon and stayed close to the Man. Moloch was near frenzy. He danced, jumped, screamed and made rude gestures.

Moloch really wasn't sure of the situation. Maybe God had given the Woman's spirit one last visit with the Man. God often did such silly, maudlin things thought Moloch. But then, he did not trust Cornelius. The angel had come with the Woman and then was gone. That was OK, but now there was another angel, a young one that Moloch had not seen before. Maybe he was an apprentice.

The movements outside by George 6234 seemed aimless. It may have made more sense to Moloch had he given the problem his full attention, but Moloch was so enraged by the presence of the Woman's spirit that he was not thinking clearly. Her goodness and grace with God were maddening to the demon whose stature was evil enough that by simple request he could have an audience with the Satan at anytime. The Woman was there too long for a simple goodbye; the presence of the second angel indicated something no good was afoot. Or more correctly, something "good" was afoot. Moloch stopped hopping around the seated man and looked around.

Something surely was amiss, but what? Moloch decided he may have foolishly discounted the presence of the Woman. He had been too sure of winning the Man without a fight after the Woman died. The young angel had drawn off to the side and was sitting in a tree. Why that tree wondered Moloch. He could find no logical reason or threat from an angel sitting in a tree. He turned his attention back to the Woman's spirit. She remained close to the Man. In fact, she had never moved from the first position she had assumed next to the Man. Moloch thought that curious. Finally, he decided it was due only to her affection for the Man and her desire for a last farewell. Yes, she could imprint her aura upon him, but once she was gone, Moloch was sure his own evilness was strong enough to beat the Man down.

Cornelius? Cornelius was the key! Where was Cornelius? Moloch was slipping in and out of moods with the flick of a tail. He finally settled down and decided, as always, Cornelius was the key. Moloch rose to the top of the building to see if he could find Cornelius. No, that wouldn't do. He should not let the Man out of his sight. He had that demonic feeling that something was amiss, but what? He decided to go back and sit next to the Man.

Moloch quickly returned to the room and sat very still, mind working and eyes scouring the area for signs of any movement or anything out of place. Ah, there. What was that? He saw movement far off in the sky; an airplane there--near the sun? The sun hurt, but it was low in the sky. Looking at it made Moloch giddy, but soon it would move below the horizon.

Cornelius had only a few precious minutes left. The Man had asked for a sign. Despite the presence of the demon Moloch, Cornelius knew that the Woman's spirit would make the Man more receptive to what Cornelius was planning. The Man had not changed position in front of the window.

The old demon was seated off to the side. Cornelius was certain that Moloch had no inkling of what was in store. The little, green demon would not be able to react in time once Cornelius acted. That was the best part of his plan. It was quick. George 6234 was sitting in a tree keeping an eye on the essential dew drop he had placed in the bush. Now was the time.

Moloch jumped up. Moloch howled. It wasn't an airplane. It was Cornelius! "What is that frog of an angel up to?" he raged.

There was no reason for Cornelius to be off up in the sky. Or was there? He was between Moloch and the sun. It didn't make sense to Moloch, and if it didn't make sense, it was dangerous. His alarm turned into instant heat. The stench was almost palpable in the room.

The Man stirred. The Woman in her spirit even noticed. Moloch had to do something. It was against the Rules, but he leaped toward the Woman's spirit.

George 6234 saw the flash of heat from Moloch and moved even as Moloch moved.

Cornelius, unaware, moved up in the sky at the same time. He refracted the light from the sun to the dew drop. It was a brilliant flash of light which steadied into a delightful sparkle.

Moloch passed in front of the Man and was reaching for the Woman's spirit. The magnified light from the dewdrop stopped him in his tracks. It hurt. He could feel the searing. Then George 6234 hit him full tilt. So much for finesse he thought. They both ended up outside in the street.

Moloch's impatience, typical of a demon, had sealed his own failure. Weakened by the magnification of the light passing through the wings of Cornelius, Moloch was easily blocked by George.

There remained for the next few months proof of their encounter--a curious scorch mark that went across the grass, sidewalk and pavement of the street.

The Man saw the light and the dewdrop sparkling. The absence of Moloch heightened the aura of the Woman's spirit.

It was a sign. The Man had asked. Heaven replied. But the Man didn't really believe. Here was the sign he asked for and he could feel the Woman's presence, but he would not believe. Cornelius allowed the sparkling light to continue until the sun disappeared below the horizon. Still the Man ignored the truth.

V

The Man wanted to believe, but also he didn't want to appear weak. Intellectualism dies hard. For too long the Man had no hope in God but only in himself. He did suspect the presence of the Woman, but was the sparkling light logical or was it a miracle? "I think you are here. The light is beautiful. Is it really you? It is so hard to believe this is not a coincidence. I need another sign."

"This is a hard case," said Cornelius. He had just arrived in the room and was talking to the Woman while looking for George 6234. He shook his head and repeated the thought, "This is a very hard case. Another Sign?"

George 6234 came dragging in. He had scorch marks and smelled of brimstone. Cornelius took one look and gave him an expectant shrug. "The little demon went after the Woman's spirit," said George 6234.

"Are you sure?"

"Without a doubt."

This was serious if true. It was a breach of the Rules. Demons, goblins, ogres and witches were evil, devious, untrustworthy, crude and downright mean, but seldom foolhardy—well, ogres were often foolhardy. The "Plan" had rules and God was supreme in enforcing those rules. The Woman's spirit was in God's Grace. She was immune to attack--no ifs, ands or buts.

Cornelius looked at the Woman and raised his eyebrows.

Her spirit had been a little faded when Cornelius came into the room but now her strength was coming back. "He scared me," she said. "You told me to ignore the little demon. But he came right at me. He grabbed for my arm just as George hit him. It was like a blindside block in football. George was just great!" She was holding up her arm and Cornelius saw a small distinctive mark that could only be made by brimstone.

"The demon will pay," growled Cornelius. Turning his attention to George he asked, "Are you all right?"

George 6234 was only an apprentice guardian angel and the full contact tackle of a journeyman demon like Moloch was dangerous indeed. He did look worn and burned; however no major injury was apparent. George 6234 had been a little faded when Cornelius came back, but his full spectrum was now returning.

The answer was expected. "I'm fine," with a big grin. "He was much more solid than I had expected. I was watching the dew drop when I noticed the little, green demon suddenly flash red. I could see the heat. The demon Moloch leaped. At first I thought he was going for the Man. Then I realized it was the Woman's spirit that was in danger. I really didn't think; I just moved. I was almost too late, but Moloch had to pass through the beam of light you refracted through the dew drop, and it stopped him momentarily--and it made him much weaker. I hit him hard--it was very hard--while he was still in the light. Somehow we ended up in the street. I came up in my best Kung Fu stance, but the little demon would have none of it. He turned his back and kind of oozed away."

"You were very fortunate," said Cornelius. "Moloch is a very ancient demon—a fallen angel in fact. He may look small--I think he does that on purpose--but he is accomplished and deadly. He has, unfortunately, bettered more than one angel. Nevertheless, you did well. I mean, you really did the right thing. Protecting the Woman, the love of God, the grace of God, was your first and only priority. I think Moloch didn't pursue the issue of your direct contact because he knew he had broken the Rules--and he will suffer for that." A movement in the lake caught Cornelius' eye.

"Moloch, you miserable toad," spoke Cornelius. It was in a low, yet clear, and ominous tone.

Moloch lolled in the lake paying no mind. He was hurting more than he thought possible, but it would not pay to let the angel see it. And it was too early to withdraw just yet.

Cornelius knew the demon heard, that Moloch was indeed watching, that the demon was still intent upon stealing the Man's soul regardless of what had passed.

"You broke the Rules, Moloch. Vile creature that you are, you still must abide by the Rules of the 'Plan'.

Jehovah God does rule. The Satan will be held accountable. You must pay."

Lucifer and his demons wanted chaos, but God would not allow chaos.

The fierceness of Cornelius' tone was unusual for an angel. Moloch had almost forgotten that Cornelius was a warrior angel. Moloch had no desire to go toe to toe with any warrior angel. Better to match wits. Now he wouldn't mind tangling again with the apprentice guardian angel, George 6234, who had only won the round because of surprise. Moloch knew he had broken the Rules.

Demons often broke the Rules. It was their nature. Actually, it is surprising they didn't break the Rules more often. Still, Jehovah God was the master of the "Plan", and rule breaking always resulted in punishment--something that really irked the fallen angels and their allies.

Lucifer, the fallen archangel who fell from grace because of his evil jealousy, was now The Great Satan. As such he fought the battle by attacking the men made in Jehovah God's image. If Lucifer could not win in direct confrontation with Jehovah God, he would ruin God's plan by attacking men.

Moloch knew that if he returned to Tartarus with a victory, if he succeeded in finally stealing the Man's soul, he could get off with only a ceremonial slap on the wrist by Lucifer. On the other hand, failure could lead to an eternity in Sheol.

It was obvious the Man's soul was now a much greater prize because of Jehovah God's direct involvement in the battle by sending Cornelius. Of course if Moloch didn't personally get punished, some other demon or goblin or witch would have to pay the full penalty for Moloch's transgression. That was the only way to balance the book. That another would suffer because of Moloch was of no concern to him. He was, after all, a demon.

Moloch realized nothing would be gained by further confrontation with Cornelius. He traveled to Tartarus and searched for Asmodeus.

VI

The Man was troubled as he looked over the pond and the bush where the crystal of light had appeared. He had slept very little the night before. He was confused. His grief was complicated by the crystal and the promise it may have held. The move from atheism to agnosticism had been easy. He saw logic there. It did not require a faith, a faith like that so strongly held by the Woman. He did respect her faith, a respect strengthened by love.

The Woman never chastised or pushed him. She had faith that someday he too would understand and accept. The friends and Cousin affected him too. They all believed, and it was a strong belief. No, it was more than a belief, he thought, it was a way of life.

The Woman had always said one day he would understand. Did she mean the crystal of light; did she know so long ago that it would come to this? No! That wasn't possible. But the coincidence--was it a coincidence?

The Man pondered as he prepared to go to the funeral home to complete the arrangements. He must hurry. The Cousin would be here soon. He thought about just being slow and late and having to rush through the day. If he had to rush, hopefully he wouldn't have time to think, to remember, to be sad, and to cry. Maybe that would make it all easier, but that wasn't his way. He was always ready and always prepared. Organization was his forte.

The funeral would be properly done. He would get through the day the way he had managed so many problems--stiff upper lip and all that. He would be in control, as always. It was of matter of pride, of mind and an intellectual exercise in self discipline.

The Man was ready when the Cousin arrived twenty minutes early. He spotted the four door Chevy immediately, and she was coming fast. He stepped off the curb, but then jumped back as she veered to the curb. The brakes squealed. Cristobal, the Cousin's guardian angel, slid off the roof where he had been riding. "I really have to work on her driving," he thought.

"I wanted to be early in case you needed help," she said to the Man.

"Our appointment is at 11 o'clock. I'm all set," he replied.

"It won't hurt to leave early. It is a long drive up there and we won't have to worry if we meet construction delays. They are tearing up Highway 287 in a few places. Do you know what you want to do about the funeral?"

"The people at the funeral home were very helpful over the telephone, and your advice was well appreciated. Let's go ahead and go now."

"So how are you doing?" she asked. She alternated between studying the Man and checking the road while driving. The traffic, fortunately, was light as she accelerated and weaved down the road. Cristobal became very attentive.

"So how are you doing?" she asked again. The Man looked OK considering the circumstances, but somewhere--psychology 101?--it said get 'em talking. Herself, she didn't want to talk. She loved and missed the Woman too. Strange, she felt it would be better for both if he were able to talk and she were able to listen.

"I'm OK," he said. "All of the out of town people are being notified. Those who need them will be sent maps. I will invite everybody to the house after the grave-side service."

"Good." There was silence for a while.

"You know, I really had a funny thing happen last night."

"Oh?" More silence. "Well?" she asked. "Don't leave me hanging with that. What funny thing last night?"

"Well, it was a light--a little crystal of light."

Her skin prickled. She grasped the steering wheel a little tighter and sat up straighter. More silence.

"Well, tell me. Don't make me pull it out of you," she demanded.

"I was sitting looking out the back window. I remembered her faith and tried to reconcile what I felt and believed with what I knew she would want me to think. It was strange. I really had some weird mood swings, like I was a beach with different waves washing up on me. I was watching the sunset thinking that was my life. Just before the sun disappeared, a bright light hit me from a bush off to the side. It was from a dewdrop in a bush. It had a brilliant crystalline clarity. It sparkled. Strange...it was warm and it gave me hope. Then it was gone."

"The Gloria."

"What?"

"The Gloria." She was so excited, she almost ran off the road. "You must be graced. You saw the Gloria...a Glory!"

"Would you be careful," he said. She was literally bouncing in the driver's seat and smiling and laughing. What was this?

"Were you praying?" she asked.

"You know better than that," was his quick reply.

"Oh?"

"Well...well I was kind of thinking out loud. I said if her faith were that strong, if there is life after death...as all of you keep telling me...." He looked at her and smiled. "I asked for a sign."

"There!"

"What do you mean, 'there'?"

"You said you asked for a sign. That light, that crystal of brightness is what you asked for. Oh, I knew it. You saw a Glory, a nimbus, an aureole; no, not an aureole, the Gloria. It was a sign, a Glory," she shouted.

"How can you be sure?"

"Faith."

"Oh, come on!"

She looked at him, left eyebrow raised, then right.

"Watch the road!" he shouted.

Amen, thought the Cousin's guardian angel, Cristobal. He had heard about the encounter with Moloch and their use of the Glory from Cornelius and George 6234. The foiled attack upon the Woman's spirit by Moloch disturbed him. Cornelius had warned that the fight for the Man's soul was apparently becoming a major skirmish--no, a "major battle" he had said--in the eternal war between good and evil. Cristobal had been asked to watch the Man as well as the Cousin during the time until the funeral. It wasn't often a non-believer was given such protection, except for small children, but Cristobal thought he understood.

Despite the light traffic, there seemed to be more demons on the road than normal. Cristobal had already intervened in a couple of instances where the Cousin wasn't careful enough driving on her own. She was more interested in the Man's story than in the road. Cristobal also wanted to influence the Cousin in her discussion with the Man about the Glory. Cornelius had said the Man was affected, yet still doubtful.

The Cousin had held many conversations with the Woman about the Man and the struggle for faith. The Woman had never despaired, but had known that faith would sometime come to the Man. It was almost like there were a pact between her and God. She knew the Man's intellectual bent, his pride and his dependence upon the mind.

"OK, let's review," the Cousin said to the Man. "You saw a light in a bush."

"It wasn't the burning bush."

"Don't get cute on me."

"Sorry," he grinned.

"Your words if I remember correctly....a bright light from the bush...from a dewdrop in the bush...brilliant crystal...sparkled. You said the bush was off to the side, not between you and the sun."

"Actually, the sun was behind the building across the lake. It hadn't set yet; it was just behind the building."

"You didn't mention that the first time."

"I just thought about it."

"It has been dry and windy. Did you ask yourself how could a dewdrop be in the bush?"

"Well, yes. After the light went out, I went and looked. I was sure it was a reflection off a can tab or sap in the bush, but it was a dew drop. And, no, I don't know how it got there."

"And you said it made you feel good."

"Yes."

"So?"

"I thought about it and asked for another sign."

"You what!" she shrieked. Cristobal was equally dismayed at the Man's words, but he was at that moment very busy keeping the car on the road while the Cousin forgot everything except the Man's awful stubbornness. Fortunately, Cristobal was not as surprised as the Cousin. He had the warning from Cornelius that the Man was a very hard case. It was all pride-- indeed!

She continued after catching her breath and steadying the car. "You have experienced a real miracle. You have seen the Gloria, a Glory just for you--just for you--and you want another sign?"

She shook her head. I am surprised, but I shouldn't be, she thought. This is a good man, but also a stubborn man. She mostly prayed while she drove the rest of the way to the funeral home.

WATCH THE ROAD !!

VII

Moloch finally found Asmodeus on a hill just north of Sarajevo. Asmodeus was in a delightful mood. Demons love misery, and there was much misery about. Moloch told him about his continuing quest to steal the Man's soul and of the intervention of Cornelius and George 6234. Moloch omitted the part about his aborted attack on the Woman's spirit. No sense in aggravating the situation with an admission of violating the rule. That information would come out soon enough he feared.

"What next?" asked Asmodeus. He knew better but he said it anyway, "I guess you'll try again...sometime?"

"I will have the Man's soul within the week. I am not going to let some sneaky angels get the best of me."

"Yeah, they ganged up on you."

Moloch let that one pass. It was after all Asmodeus who had abandoned him in a silly fit of pique over a small misunderstanding. It had been stupid of Asmodeus to look for the Man all that time in Tennessee. Asmodeus should have just found Moloch. He knew Moloch would be where the Man was. Or, maybe the senior demon had hoped to take the prize himself--alone--while Moloch was elsewhere.

Asmodeus had reveled in the other's failure as the story was told. He had always considered the older demon a potent rival for Lucifer's favor. Sure they cooperated from time to time, but only when Asmodeus felt such cooperation was to his own personal advantage. He suspected this was going to become a major effort.

Asmodeus knew of and respected Cornelius. No, “respect” was the wrong word. He feared Cornelius. Demons respected no one and no thing, but they did know fear. Asmodeus decided he just might help Moloch out. Serbia and Croatia were fun but too easy...stupid men were no challenge. Yes he'd go with Moloch and do battle with the angels for one good soul. There just may be a personal benefit to be gained at Moloch’s expense.

"I'll see you at the funeral," said Moloch. "You'll be there?"

"I wouldn't miss it."

Moloch nodded, wondering if Asmodeus also had to go to Denver. Probably. Denver was going to be a big deal, and Lucifer wanted to create mayhem! Moloch had seen the New York Times article:

Pope John Paul II announced plans today to visit Denver, which he said he had selected as the site of a world youth conference next year.

The Pope, who last visited the United States in 1987, said after celebrating Mass in Vatican City that the conference would take place in August 1993. Buffalo and Minneapolis-St. Paul had also sought the weeklong event, which is expected to draw 100,000 people.

A statement by Roman Catholic bishops in the United States said Denver was an attractive location for Hispanic people in the southwestern United States and Central America. Surveys indicate the Catholic Church in the United States will be 50 percent Hispanic by 2020.

Denver has about 275,000 Hispanic residents, the largest Hispanic population of the three cities considered for the conference. Its Catholic population is estimated at 330,000.

"I have selected the city of Denver, in the noted Rocky Mountains, in the state of Colorado, which has not been included on the itinerary of my previous apostolic trips" to the United States, the Pope told 30,000 worshipers at an outdoor Palm Sunday Mass.

Denver! Lucifer had said, "Denver first, the Man's soul second."

Moloch was not happy about the interruption in his quest for the Man's soul, but go to Denver he must. It was because of that Christian meeting called World Youth Day. He remembered it was held every two years and Moloch had been to the last one in Argentina. Youth from around the world made a pilgrimage to a site selected by the Pope who lived in Rome. This time the Pope had picked Denver and over 300,000 Christians were expected to be there. The Pope would travel there too. Lucifer hated such gatherings with their aura of faith and prayer. While it was of little use to harass such faithful as these, Lucifer, The Satan, was not willing to let such occasions go without confrontation. It was a "matter of principle." Moloch had heard that more than once and barely suppressed a snicker each time the lofty words were uttered by The Dragon. "Since when did evil have principle?" he wondered.

Moloch would go to Denver as ordered, but first he would visit Ahrim who owed him a favor.

VIII

"Asmodeus."

Asmodeus was deep in thought. He was weighing the chance of success in assisting Moloch to steal the Man's soul. How much of the credit could he, Asmodeus, wrest from Moloch if the Man's soul were won? How much help was Cornelius going to get from Jehovah God? Bottom line--was the reward worth the effort; or maybe, better said, was the reward worth the RISK? It was Moloch's game. Asmodeus was sure he could successfully stab the finger of blame at Moloch if there were another failure. Asmodeus was good at that. But then certainly Moloch....

"Asmodeus!"

Lucifer was calling. Asmodeus heard the impatience and jumped up flying to the great Satan.

"Master?"

"Denver!"

"Denver? Snakes and caldrons," he thought, "I've been so busy trying to ace out Moloch I forgot about Denver."

For the good and pious, things were not going that well in Denver. Evil was on the upswing. Many forces not directly allied with Lucifer appeared to be helping in his work there--and Lucifer already had many demons, ogres and witches in the city. Gangs were increasing their wanton street violence; new age religions were flourishing; shamanism was getting more and more favorable press; and there were even pockets of Satanism--happy times! But, the Pope was coming to Denver.

Baba was supposed to keep the Pope occupied with genocide in Yugoslavia. Baba, a witch who often left Tartarus to live in a hut deep in the woods of Eastern Europe, was always close behind the four horsemen. She had a hideous countenance. Prominent were her ragged teeth made of iron. Rumors, never proven, were that she stole and ate small children. Still, there were those neat piles of small bones found in the dark forests.... An icon of wickedness and evil and a minion of Lucifer, Baba's efforts in Serbia and Croatia were getting less success. Western nations had intervened, and the Pope was able to attend other, long scheduled events.

The Pope being in Denver could ruin everything that was planned by Lucifer there. And Asmodeus could visualize the finger of guilt pointed directly at himself. Asmodeus did not like the Pope, but then he never saw a Pope he did like. This one was particularly bothersome however. The Pope had ruined The Satan's great plan in the communist east. A Polish Pope. They should have stopped him at the very beginning. But they couldn't. The dark forces were lacking. Many demons paid for that miscalculation. Then the assassination had been planned and that had failed...so close. Asmodeus could not understand how the assassination attempt on the Pope had failed, but he was very glad he was meddling in Chile at the time. Lucifer had laid the groundwork for the Pope's assassination himself, but then as he always did with risky schemes that could result in direct confrontation with Jehovah, Lucifer left the details to an underling; in this case, Waverlot. The scheme failed and Waverlot was quickly banished to Sheol for eternity. That was Lucifer's way of saying, "Not me!"

"Ahhhh...I was on my way to Denver when you called, Master." Asmodeus could not look Lucifer in the eye. The lie came easy. Then a thought. "Perhaps Master, I could take Moloch with me?"

"You were supposed to be there to help with the goblins before the Pope arrived. Temptation 16 is losing control of the situation. Go!"

Asmodeus was happy to escape from his forgetfulness so easily, but then he was more than a little dismayed at the prospect of going where so many angels would be hovering. Nor was he keen on helping out Temptation 16. That was one demon that got too much bad press and he was a potent rival of Asmodeus. Since Lucifer had not said yes or no about Moloch, Asmodeus would take him along anyway.

"Moloch is there already," toned the Dragon with a smile. The unbidden information was unnerving.

Asmodeus was always a little anxious that Lucifer could invade his thoughts at will.

Asmodeus met Temptation 16 and Moloch on the gold dome of Colorado's Capitol building. Before they got down to business they took a break and caressed and slavered over the yellow metal on the dome, almost getting a high from the smell of greed the precious substance emanated.

"It is not going well," said Temptation 16. "It's not just that there are too many angels about, there are too many good people. I send demons into the groups of pilgrims but then I have to pull the demons out early because they get faint and weak. The goblins can't concentrate; they just flit about. The ogres are almost useless in such a strong environment of faith. They are too lazy and uncontrollable because unlike the witches they have no souls to lose. I would give ten ogres for one good demon, but Lucifer diverted all the extra demons to the Middle East and Africa. We appear to be losing ground there."

He continued while stroking the gold on the Capitol dome, "We have tried to strengthen our new, human allies who are protesting and generally making loud noises against the Pope. Jealousy 3 is working with them--.giving encouragement, whispering hate and suggestions.

Her efforts have been monumental, but our earthly 'friends' are weak."

Temptation 16 then went into a long review of specific actions attempted against the Pope and his pilgrims, some successful, but most of which had failed.

After a long, hissing discussion, being careful the overflying angels could not hear, the three demons finally reached uncommon agreement. They would worry less about disrupting the Pope and corrupting his followers but would work harder on maintaining their gains already made in Denver. They took all of the ogres and half the demons and witches and sent them again into Denver and its suburbs. The goblins, remaining half of demons and witches were told to stay near the Pope's pilgrims to capitalize on any targets of opportunity. After a full review, they realized this was probably a futile gesture, but one that would be demanded by Lucifer who insisted there were always possibilities for mayhem and the stealing of souls.

The three demons divided their time between their forces in Denver and its suburbs and those looking for opportunity against the Pope. They wanted to at least maintain the level of evil which Temptation 16 had achieved so far in this hot summer. They made the gold dome their headquarters and controlled the action from there--all under the watchful eye of a legion of angels who thwarted many of their forays.

"The Man," Asmodeus asked Moloch, "anything new?"

Moloch was not happy. He had not wanted to come to Denver. As far as he was concerned, the battle for the Man's soul was far from over. Moloch was sure his only guarantee of success against Cornelius and the other angels was to stay near the Man, but Lucifer, who was never understanding, sneered at the possibility of another failure. He insisted that Moloch help Temptation 16 in

Denver. Moloch had no problem helping Temptation 16 fight the Pope; this just was not the best time. First the failure with the Man and now he was sure his alliance with Temptation 16 was going to result in another failure. Being unable to seriously disrupt the Pope and his Pilgrims would set him back even more with Lucifer. And it was a matter of pride. He was going to steal the Man's soul. It had all seemed so easy in the beginning--and even the second time. Being overconfident, Moloch had boasted too much to too many. Lucifer had warned him; he must see this battle for the Man's soul to a successful conclusion.

Lucifer finally allowed an anxious Moloch to leave Denver, but first Moloch was to check with Asmodeus.

"Is not the Woman's funeral tomorrow?" asked Asmodeus

"It is delayed," replied Moloch.

Moloch had been fortunate in finding Ahrim, an up and coming demon, who was available because he was recovering from what he called a "small altercation" with a group of warrior angels over Nigeria. At Moloch's request, Ahrim was able to cause several scheduling errors at the funeral home in Memphis. He caused the funeral to be delayed three days so it would not coincide with the time Moloch had to be in Denver.

"Tomorrow and I must be there," Moloch replied. "That will be the Man's weakest time. He has had time to think and doubt. Temptation 16 has agreed to go with me. We will both be there. The Man is stubborn and confused with grief. As you know, Cornelius created a miracle and gave the Man a sign. The Man believed, but then wanted another sign. We will take advantage of his foolish pride. We will not only ensure that there are no more signs, but we will inflict greater feelings of grief and loss upon the Man. We will magnify the loss by encouraging mourners and friends to extol the Woman's virtues. We will accentuate for the Man the unfairness of the loss--not just to him but to his children and friends. We will whisper that the Woman abandoned him on purpose—that she wanted to leave to be with Jehovah. We will move the Man farther away from the good influence exerted by the departed Woman. We may not win his soul tomorrow, but he will be so weakened by the loss that he will never profess love of Jehovah God. We will get the Man to curse Him."

"And Cornelius?" Asmodeus could see his question was unsettling. "Do you want me to handle Cornelius?"

Moloch was immediately wary. An offer of help was something seldom extended by a fellow demon, a goblin seeking favor maybe, but not a fellow demon. Demons were too ambitious--too self centered. An ogre might offer to help, but they were in it for the fun--and any illegitimate spilling of blood that could be sniffed up. But an offer of help from Asmodeus was not to be taken lightly. Given the senior demon's position Moloch could not refuse even though he was tempted. Still, he knew Cornelius would be there, as would George 6234. Asmodeus would be in this only for personal gain, but if there were trouble again it would be nice to have a more powerful demon to help with it--and share in any blame if it came to that. But Moloch was optimistic and he planned to feast upon the Man's soul. He was suffering from a devilish combination of pride, greed and blood lust.

"I want that Man. You take care of Cornelius" was his delayed reply to Asmodeus.

Giving only a brief thought to Moloch's answer, Asmodeus pretended to be helpful in his response. "The Pope leaves tonight. You can go to Memphis now. Temptation 16 and Jealousy will help me with the last few disruptions."

Moloch didn't even take the time to reply. He was gone the instant Asmodeus gave leave. There must be no mistakes tomorrow. Jehovah's humans were curiously vulnerable at funerals, and if handled right he could have the Man's soul by sundown. Moloch planned on being at the Man's side whispering and cajoling him into blasphemy and renunciation. Given the angels' interference last time, Moloch knew it would be another fight. He decided Asmodeus' offer to handle Cornelius might not be a bad thing after all. Asmodeus hated Cornelius as much as Moloch did and was certain to bring as many demons along as possible--many more than Moloch could have persuaded Lucifer to allow, given the unexpected softening of the situation in the Middle East. Stupid humans, they were so unpredictable!

Little did Moloch realize that this little fight for one man's soul was going to escalate into a major battle.

Moloch wanted that Man's soul. Asmodeus would have his hands full if Cornelius showed up as Moloch expected. Moloch doubted Asmodeus would gain a significant victory over Cornelius and he did not care. He just wanted both of them kept busy while he stole the Man's soul. The game was: no credit for Asmodeus and no interference from Cornelius. While Asmodeus was engaged in fruitless maneuvering against Cornelius, Moloch would triumphantly, personally deliver the soul to The Dragon--after Moloch himself had feasted on it—just a little. His grisly smile dripped at the thought.

IX

Cristobal had remained in Memphis dividing his time between the Cousin and the Man. He should have known better but he had been overly encouraged by the angels' successful efforts making the Man see the sign, the Gloria--the flash of light from the bush and the lightly felt presence of the Woman's spirit--all done right under Moloch's nose. The Man's reaction while disappointing was not so uncommon for humans--frustrating, but not discouraging. Cristobal was at first surprised Moloch had left and that no other demon replaced him, hoping maybe Moloch's transgression in attacking the Woman's spirit would end the attempt at the Man. But then demons never did anything for the right reason, and Moloch probably would be back. It was obvious that Moloch wanted that Man's soul--badly.

Cristobal would make sure the Cousin was near the Man as much as possible the day the funeral was held. He was certain the Friend and her guardian angel would be available that day also, and probably a few more. Cristobal had that feeling they would need all the angels they could get.

The Cousin was worried. The Man had seen the sign; he had felt the sign. It was so like him to expect another sign and then make his decision on its presence or absence. He's a good man, she told herself, but stubborn. Too often he went with logic and not with the heart. She and the Woman had discussed this flaw many times. Humility was not his strong point but they both knew many people who had much worse and many more flaws. The Cousin stayed by the Man. Her goodness helped the Man, and Cristobal did all he could to strengthen the positive aura.

The Man had loved the Woman. He still loved her. He wanted to believe they could be together again—wherever and whenever. He had been buoyed by the sign and the touch of her spirit, but too many years of doubting had made it hard to realize and accept the miracle.

"One is a coincidence," he whispered. "Two is a sign."

The day of the funeral started with a brilliant sunrise and clear blue skies. Moloch listened to the weather report and his normally morose mood became even fouler--he was worried. He didn't like it. "Clear" in the morning was good, but the afternoon had to be cloudy for his plan to work. He had set events in motion. He could only hope he had fooled both the angels and the weather man.

Moloch was having trouble staying in the shadows. The higher the sun rose the more it hurt. He sensed an ominous omen. But then ominous omens were for men and he was a demon. He would do his best to make this a day of gloom and doom for the Man.

"Well?" Asmodeus had arrived. "Cristobal is here...and Cornelius?"

"He's about," Moloch replied. "I haven't seen him, but I can feel him. I feel droopy. I'm sure he caused this pretty day. I feel worse than droopy. We must do something soon. I left a skulk of ogres at the town water tower.

Asmodeus interrupted, "You have a plan?" This last was said with more than a little malice and condescension from the senior demon. Asmodeus was letting his jealously of Moloch interfere. Moloch an older, yet lower ranked demon, had unusually open access to Lucifer. Asmodeus knew if their operation succeeded, Moloch would receive the accolades. His fear was that should they fail, he Asmodeus would somehow get the blame."

"I know how to handle Cristobal," said Moloch. "You take care of Cornelius. I'll need extra demons to harass the Cousin and the guests at the funeral. The guests almost without exception are Christians--strong Christians--ugh! The aura of faith is going to be sick...sickening. I plan to change the weather. I want fire and brimstone, but I'll settle for rain, wind and lightning. Thunderstorm clouds will do. Not too close to the cemetery, but close enough that we can move them in during the funeral. I want it dark and foreboding with demons dancing on all the graves. I want those Christians to see nothing but lightning and hear nothing but thunder and feel nothing but wind and rain. I want them to feel and fear death. Cristobal is the Cousin's guardian angel. He must feel the need to spend all his time protecting her and thus ignore the Man. Extra demons must be assigned to her. I'll take any ogres we can get. Their banshee howling will help while I wheedle and whipsaw the Man into a grief-stricken frenzy of blasphemy and denouncement of everything the Woman believed. Then I will steal his soul. Yes! His soul will be mine!"

"You're the boss here," said Asmodeus. Under normal circumstances; Moloch would have been happy to have heard such a concession, but this was not a good situation. He suspected and feared some kind of treachery from Asmodeus. He knew Asmodeus was setting the record straight in case Moloch failed to steal the soul. Asmodeus could always claim his part was only to distract Cornelius—the required level of distraction forever open to interpretation.

X

Cornelius had returned to Heaven after the struggle for the Man's soul. Moloch's transgression against the Woman's spirit had to be recorded in the Judgment Day Book. In telling his story to Gabriel, ever remembering the frailty of humankind, he decided he could only keep his perspective by using men's humor.

"You know the current humor of men," he reminded Gabriel. "The good news--bad news thing. Well the good news is that despite the slimy little demon's foul deeds, including the attack on the Woman's spirit, Moloch did not steal the Man's soul. The bad news is that despite our Gloria, and the help of the Woman's spirit, the Man is not yet won. He is not safe from Moloch and his kindred evil spirits.

Gabriel replied, "The Man must be protected and ultimately won for Jehovah. It is part of the Plan. It was providential that Asmodeus was not there. I understand he was supposed to help Moloch, but they had a falling out...typical demons."

"I agree. Moloch was a handful by himself. Oh, did I mention that George 6234 was an able assistant. No…he was more than that. When Moloch attacked the Woman's spirit, George 6234 saved her. By her accounting, he did an incredible job."

Gabriel was thoughtful. Then he asked, "Is it over, or do you think Moloch will continue his quest for the soul?"

"This is not the first time Moloch has been after the Man's soul. Many years ago Moloch apparently had found the Man to be a tempting target but considered him such an easy mark he delayed to seek a more challenging victim. His failure to quickly win an easy soul led to some serious trouble with the Satan. After some time, Moloch then decided to correct his mistake and erase, so to speak, his failure."

"In the interval," Cornelius continued, "The Man met the Woman. I was her guardian angel. It was one of those rare cases where her goodness protected him. Moloch came around for his prize and was sorely surprised to find the Man's situation to be entirely changed. A good woman with a guardian angel was on the scene."

"Unfortunately, Moloch's arrival coincided with an unexpected and tragic loss of his twin brother by the Man. They were far from home in Okinawa at the time. The Man was flying jet fighters for the Air Force. Without faith, the Man took the loss very hard. He strayed from the Woman's influence and thus weakened my ability to help him."

"Moloch apparently decided the time was again ripe for soul stealing and didn't want to miss the second opportunity. Somehow he managed to get Asmodeus involved. I believe Asmodeus was in Okinawa stirring up the Communist separatists and trying to blockade the American bases with riots—any cause to produce terror and bloodshed."

"Together they worked on a plane crash in their plan to steal the Man's soul. It was supposed to crash into a Japanese school—more bloodshed, more riots, more terror from an evil plan. It was by Grace that I was able to change the Man's plane from one with a single pilot to a training version with two pilots. The other pilot had a guardian angel, Franciscus.

"Aahh... I remember the story now," laughed Gabriel. "Franciscus has told it to me many times. It is a very entertaining story. Those two demons must really have been surprised to find two guardian angels watching that airplane. Rumor is that Moloch and Asmodeus were at odds with each other long after. If they are together again after the same soul, you will need help. Those demons will be more difficult to defeat a second time."

"I agree. That time with the plane, it was a struggle for control of the situation," remembered Cornelius. "There was no direct contact between angel and demon then. Now, with Moloch's attack on the Woman's spirit, I see the battle is escalating. Moloch has failed to steal the Man's soul two times now."

"I think we could agree that Asmodeus is a two-time loser as well," added Gabriel. "Moloch's violation of the Rule by attacking the Woman's spirit would certainly go easier with Lucifer if he could finally bring in the Man's soul. The demons will see a final victory after so many failures as increasing the soul's worth many times."

"This could get really serious," advised Gabriel. "Who do you have helping now?"

"Cristobal is the Cousin's guardian angel. The Cousin has stayed very close to the Man in his time of grief. George 6234 is with me for training...he is a jewel. The Friend and her guardian angel, Mercy 1021, can also be counted on. The Woman had many Christian friends so I expect more angels at the funeral. I am not sure who they would be right now, but I believe our next problem will certainly be at the funeral."

"When is that scheduled?" asked the Archangel.

"In two days," replied Cristobal. "Moloch had earlier managed some mischief which resulted in a three day delay. Otherwise he would have been in Denver during the funeral. Lucifer made him go to Denver to help the other demons planning chaos and malevolent disruptions during the Papal visit there. After the Pope leaves Denver, I'm sure Moloch will be allowed to return to Memphis to continue his wicked quest."

"That three day delay is evidence of continuing interest by the Throne in Tartarus. I'm not surprised. This one is important," said Gabriel. "I'm certain Asmodeus will be there too--and maybe some other demons from their Denver foray."

The Archangel continued, "I'll have one legion of angels on call just for St. Agnes. She is watching over Los Angeles right now, but she can be there to help you in a flash."

St. Agnes, known for her beauty in Rome and martyred in the year 304 at age 13 had developed into a most suitable commander of an Angel Legion under the tutelage of Michael.

After his meeting with Gabriel, Cornelius did some serious planning. He decided that the second sign for the Man would again be a Gloria. The Man had already seen one and should have no difficulty in recognizing another--and no difficulty in accepting it this time, but still the angel was worried. Cornelius went back to Gabriel and secured permission for the Woman's spirit to be at the funeral. George 6234 would also be at her side.

The morning of the funeral, Moloch was in the corner of the room when the Man woke up. Moloch had joined a couple of ogres he had put there all night with instructions to disturb the Man's sleep with sighing, wailing and snapping. Then with the skillful use of some soapy moisture Moloch had even managed a small shock from the Man's electric shaver. That resulted in a dropped and broken shaver. A gleeful Moloch had been working on tainted food when the Cousin showed up with her Guardian Angel, Cristobal. Moloch was gone in a flash, leaving the poor ogres to Cristobal's wrath.

The mood at the funeral home was somber yet expectant. The Christians were happy and sad--sad that the Woman had left them and her family, but happy that she was "going home" to be with Jehovah God. Their faith buoyed up the assembled friends and family.

The Man, having no faith, was disconsolate, yet he also had a little expectancy tugging at his doubts. It would be decided--sign or coincidence? He wouldn't admit he wanted to believe, not to himself, not to anyone, but the Cousin and the friends were so sure about the Glory. Their faith had no logic and, so in a way, was all the more wondrous.

That morning Cornelius had picked up George 6234 and dropped in at the funeral home for a quick advisement of the other angels.

"Gabriel and I have discussed the situation. We agree on the likelihood of a major battle for the Man's soul. I have at my disposal a legion of angels with another in reserve.

"Moloch and Asmodeus are certain to be among our adversaries...certainly the prime players. How many more demons and who they are will help give a clue to how seriously the crowd in Tartarus is taking this. We don't think Lucifer will be directly involved, because right now he is overseeing hideous crimes in so many other major areas around the world. Still, we must be prepared for a phalanx of demons."

Cristobal replied. "We agree. Mercy 1021 and I talked it over yesterday after the Friend arrived. We didn't realize the extent of the threat, but we are certain Moloch is planning more deviltry. We weren't sure whether to expect trouble at the funeral home and chapel service or at the cemetery. The funeral motorcade is a possibility, but we agreed Moloch couldn't expect major results from ruining that part of the day."

After much discussion among the angels it was agreed the most probable site for a venture by Moloch was the cemetery, at graveside. That fit into a plan that Cornelius was formulating for he and Gabriel had earlier reached the same conclusion.

"Remember, my friends," he said, "our goal is not just to defeat Lucifer and his demons, but to save the Man's soul and lead him into a state of Grace. To do that we must not only thwart the plans of Moloch and Asmodeus but we must give the Man the sign he is seeking."

"George 6234, you stay here with Cristobal and watch for Moloch," advised the senior angel. "I will bring the Woman's spirit to the cemetery. At that time you must always be with her."

Cornelius then went to the cemetery to check the situation there. Too many demons about for a sunny day was his immediate observation. They were just lazing about telling ogre jokes. Cornelius felt the attack had to come at the cemetery. More and more demons were just casually dropping by to sit on gravestones. And he thought he saw the shadow of Asmodeus. That really meant trouble. He had advised Cristobal and the other angels that the cemetery was the probable target, but nevertheless to be on their toes (Wings?) at the funeral home in case Moloch tried something there, if only a diversion. And where was Moloch?

XI

Moloch had dropped by the funeral home. Those in attendance were solemn, yet it was clear hope and faith were abundant. Moloch growled. He did not like it. The chapel was filled not only with people, but guardian angels were hovering about as well. Cristobal, of course, was there, and Mercy 1021, the Friend's guardian angel who had also been at the Hospital when the Woman died. Moloch thought about calling in more reinforcements—maybe a skulk of goblins or two. But goblins were almost harder to control than ogres.

Moloch found the atmosphere stifling. Where did all these Christians come from he wondered. Sure it was the Bible belt, but still....Yes it would be best to work in the open spaces of the cemetery. Funeral homes sometimes were okay for causing trouble, but not this time. He thought about sending in a few ogres for a diversion. He discarded the idea after counting the angels present and realizing that ogres really wouldn't be effective, even as a diversion, without some serious oversight. Moloch didn't want to take away from the all important battle at the cemetery. Yes, it probably would be a battle if Cornelius were still around. Warrior angels weren't to be trifled with, but he was going to go all out to win that one soul--even if the fight erupted into a dangerous battle--and let the Devil take the hindmost--as long as it wasn't him.

Still, Moloch felt he shouldn't ignore the Man and the funeral service altogether. Moloch's absence or failure to at least make an appearance would only result in the angels being certain he intended mischief elsewhere. Also, part of his plan was to keep the Man off balance the whole day. He'd started with an early morning of mean pranks--at least until Cristobal had showed up. He must continue the program. He had to counter all that messy good will the Cousin and friends were directing at the Man. Besides, done right, it would only take a moment and the skins of a few expendable ogres. After this change of mind, he called to the skulk of ogres Asmodeus had left waiting by the water tower.

"I want you to go sit on the coffin when they sing the first song," he directed the ogres. One ogre, for the fun of it, had moved through the chapel on her way to Moloch and had seen the angels. She almost didn't recover from the shock.

"The angels...," she began. The other ogres jumped as if all were tied to a single cord.

"Dare you question me?" growled Moloch. The brimstone made their eyes water. "The first song—remember. Go!" Cowering, the ogres retreated to wait at the base of the water tower. Presently, the smallest of the lot was dispatched to watch and give the signal when the first song of the funeral service began.

Moloch then called three minor demons lounging about the cemetery. "Your task is simple. I want you to play tag among the cars outside the funeral home. Start when the first song is sung by those inside. You must go through the limousine or hearse every third time. Wait at the water tower with the ogres--and keep them in line!"

The demons caterwauled and howled. They didn't like ogres--but then who did? "No one can control ogres," said one.

"GO!" commanded Moloch. His forked tail whipped viciously through the air.

The demons left with no attempt to muffle their grumbling.

It was obvious the combination of heavy prayer from the Christians and the presence of the angels were disturbing the forces of evil.

Moloch went to the Memphis town jail and waited. He would be out of the way of nosy angels and at the same time energize himself with this local source of misery.

The ogres were not happy to see the demons come to "their" water tower. Before their natural bickering erupted into a real fight, Moloch's plan was saved by the start of the funeral service and the first song. Hearing the initial notes of the chapel organ, the ogres rushed into the funeral chapel. Forgetting their previous fears about the angels they clawed each other out of the way playing "king of the mountain" on the casket.

Moloch heard the clamor of the ogres as they stampeded by to see who could be first on the casket.

Hurrying from the jail, he passed the demons as they started to play tag on the cars.

The angels were quick to recover from the shock of the onslaught by oily, evil creatures and their sordid chatter in the funeral home. The angels made quick work of driving off the ogres with a scattering of ogre limbs and pieces thrown around. As the angels turned their attention to the three demons in the cars, Moloch moved beside the Man.

"Sheol!" he cried. A stupid blunder. The Man was unmoved by Moloch's presence as the congregation filled the small chapel with "Amazing Grace." Moloch hadn't been thinking right. The power of the song blunted his evil. Time was short, what to do? He must leave a mark on this miserable human. Moloch hopped on the Man's shoulders in an effort to increase the burden of sadness and loss. Then Moloch, sensing the fast closing presence of Cristobal, brayed obscenities and was gone.

Moloch found Asmodeus at the cemetery. "Have you seen Cornelius?" asked Moloch.

"Yes, and Cristobal—is he about?"

"Cristobal is at the funeral home. I left him something to think about. I'm more worried about Cornelius. Has he seen you?"

"I don't know. I've tried to stay in the shadows."

"Let's get out of here. I told Temptation 16 we'd meet him on the water tower." The two demons flew to the water tower. Moloch realized too late it was a poor choice for such a sunny day. They were both wilting by the time they got there.

Temptation 16 was nowhere to be seen. An ogre was on the top of the tower's unlighted Christmas star trying to look like a chicken hawk but not being very successful.

"Have you seen Temptation?" asked Moloch.

"Which one?" replied the ogre chicken hawk.

Moloch ground his teeth until sparks flew. He looked at Asmodeus who just shrugged. Ogres were a bother. Demons were never really sure whether ogres were there to help or hinder—maybe a bad joke by Jehovah. The real problem was that Moloch was bad with numbers and all Temptation demons had numbers. There were just too many Temptations.

Moloch answered with a guess, "Temptation 6."

"Haven't seen him."

Normally green, Moloch turned brilliant red and let out a howl that sounded so much like the town siren that the volunteer fire department responded to the false alarm.

Asmodeus watched the firemen run helter and skelter, trying to figure out what was wrong. He was enjoying their confusion--silly humans--and was tempted to do more mischief. Moloch's heat brought him back to the problem at hand.

Asmodeus decided he'd better get involved in the matter. A flare-up by Moloch right now would not be helpful. It would weaken Moloch and it would cause more attention than they wanted right now. Ogres were just plain dumb as well as ornery, but you had to know how to handle them. "Why are you here?" he asked the ogre.

"Huh?"

"Why are YOU here?" The tone was not nice.

The ogre replied in a squeak, "Temptation asked me to wait here for two demons."

"Temptation who?" Asmodeus noted the ogre's discomfort with satisfaction.

"Temptation 16."

"And what were you to do if two demons came by?"

The ogre was slow, but not completely stupid. His answer was direct. "To tell them—you-- he's in the sewer down there."--pointing.

Moloch was almost delirious from the sun and his anger. He was in the sewer in a flash. "Temptation 16, where did you find that ogre?" he snarled. "Why weren't you at the water tower?"

Asmodeus watched with pleasure. The other's discomfort felt good. And, he preferred that the two other demons not get too friendly with each other, although such really wasn't too likely in any event.

Temptation 16 wasn't the newest demon on the block so he cared little about Moloch's wrath even though he enjoyed the warmth thrown off by the other's anger.

"Come on, Moloch, you know that water tower was a stupid place to meet in broad sunlight! Why didn't you dim the sunlight? I thought you wanted a storm for this funeral. As for the ogre, who cares about ogres?"

Asmodeus quickly broke in, "What's the plan?"

Moloch had to get control of himself. This obsession with the Man's soul was making his normal foul mood even worse, and he needed these demons' help. Either one could leave in a huff at the flick of an ear. Asmodeus had already proved that once before.

He explained, "The service has just started at the funeral home. It will last sixty to ninety minutes. The drive to the cemetery is another sixty minutes. I don't like sunshine anymore than you do, but today we need it; we need sunshine this morning at least.

"We need the sun for thermal convection; we need to make clouds--thunderstorm clouds. Because I had to be in Denver, I didn't have time to bring in a warm or cold front for the bad weather we need. Besides, the angels could easily see us manipulating the weather if we tried to move a whole weather system. I don't want to be so obvious. If we can get a thunderstorm to occur 'naturally' we can augment it at the last minute and move it over the cemetery. Experience has proven that a storm will naturally reduce men's spirits. It is just another edge I want when I steal the Man's soul. Combine the storm's real danger with demons, ogres and goblins and the angels will be too busy with the other humans to think about the Man."

"It sounds complicated; is a storm really necessary?" asked Temptation 16. "That seems chancy. Why not just overwhelm them with numbers? We have many goblins and ogres available."

Moloch hesitated. He was entering into an area of discussion that followers of Lucifer naturally avoided. It involved a subject most unpleasant to The Dragon--miracles and the Spirit.

He responded, "There is another problem--the light. I don't want any sunlight. Remember the miracle I told you about. They almost won the Man last time with some sunlight and a piece of dew. The Jehovah God's faithful call it a Glory, a Gloria. It is a burst of light and is very powerful. It carries the Spirit. Only the Man's stubbornness kept it from succeeding. I can use that stubbornness to my advantage, but we need the storm to execute our plan."

The others were mute for a long time. Finally, Asmodeus asked, "This 'natural' thunderstorm, how are you going to do that? Surely the angels will be suspicious."

"No, storms are not uncommon this time of year. The monsoon flow from the Baja Gulf is late this season and there is plenty of moisture plus warmer air moving in. The upper atmosphere is a little cooler. We have a good unstable mix just for starters—the warm air moves up, the cold air moves down. In addition to the general warm-up from the sun, we add some strong local thermal heating for a great storm. It's going to be fun when we start adding some brimstone vapors to the thunder and lightning....Hmmm, I wonder how big I can get the hail."

"You're making this weather; in two hours?" Temptation 16 was almost snorting in derision. He was still smarting from the failure in Denver. Moloch hadn't been much help there; he'd been too involved in making plans to steal this soul in Memphis.

"We started the day the Woman died. Look to the west," pointed Moloch.

The other two demons looked and saw clouds were already forming in the blue sky. Moloch pointed out two that were thicker and taller than the rest. One was southwest and the other, a little farther away was directly west over some smoke.

"Your smoke?" asked Asmodeus.

"Yes. Well, actually, the credit goes to Ahrim." Moloch was pleased to see the surprised looks from the other two demons. Ahrim was an up-and-coming demon, a ward of Ahriman, one of the oldest and most powerful of the fallen angels in Tartarus. Ahrim, one of the best at new age evil, had studied hard under Ahriman and eventually exceeded even the old master in mayhem and chaos. He was known for his cruelty to lost souls. Moloch gained new stature in the eyes of Asmodeus and Temptation having Ahrim as an ally.

MEMPHIS
"CHICKEN HAWK" OGRE WAITING ON TWO DEMONS

XII

Moloch had been lucky. Ahrim had said he wasn't too busy to return the favor he owed Moloch. Ahrim was still recovering from a head to head confrontation with the Archangel Gabriel. Moloch couldn't remember all the particulars of the fight--and it was a fight. Ahrim was involved in the plans to assassinate the Pope--but only because Lucifer was personally interested in the plot. Somewhere along the line, a confrontation with Gabriel occurred. Ahrim had been victor in too many evil successes in the 20th century wars. It made him just a little too cocky. Always a hero to the demons, he allowed their obsequious adoration to temper reason when he and Gabriel faced-off. Moloch was told the story by the demon "Loy, The Elder."

As Loy told it, "Ahrim was on the march with two phalanxes of demons, a coven of witches and a skulk of goblins when Gabriel hovered to their front.

"Far enough," said Gabriel, "'Jehovah God rules."

"The demons howled, frothed and snapped. Gabriel was unfazed, but assumed that look warrior angels get.

He didn't look mad or mean. His appearance was of one unconcerned, almost sad. Ahrim was at first uncertain, but the pack instinct of the demons--who were of course behind him--caused him to utter a horrible oath and charge the angel without notice. No doubt Gabriel was surprised. Most in the underworld had long ago given up one-on-one combat. He was slow to move and took a brimstone burn on the left wing.

"Ahrim stopped and turned. His success on the first rush left him heady. He sneered and sharpened his claws. He saw Gabriel's aura flicker and smiled a bloody smile.

"Angel," he hissed, "you will be my trophy."

Loy, The Elder, had continued the story, eyes again seeing what had happened long before, "The two phalanxes of demons boiled and roared. They moved to be again behind Ahrim. Unfortunately for Ahrim, he failed to notice the angel's aura had returned stronger. Gabriel hovered inches off the ground and waited. The demon spat at the angel who only watched. Ahrim then uttered a series of blasphemies and sparked a bolt of fire. The angel remained as before, making no sound."

Loy, The Elder, finished the story in a coarse whisper. "The skulk of goblins started to spread out to encircle the angel. They were joined by a few witches. Cymbals rang out. The phalanxes of the demons became deadly quiet as they wheeled into attack formation. The goblins increased their volume tenfold. Their own frenzy was such that they even nipped each other. Ahrim's shadow was getting darker and darker. His taunting voice was that of a thousand death chants. The pack added their chorus. The angel slowed his flight and touched earth. The constant roar of sound appeared to unnerve him."

"Ahrim gestured to the lead phalanx of demons and he charged. But he charged alone. The demons, displaying an unusual temerity, were uncertain of easy victory against an archangel and they hung back. Not that it made any difference. Gabriel moved ever so slightly it seemed; and Ahrim…was gone! No noise, no light, no blows, no nothing. All that remained of the encounter was a small rent at the bottom of Gabriel's robe and the disappearing wail of a fallen angel falling again."

Loy continued, "The damage to Ahrim was so bad he even spent time in Sheol hoping the utter desolation would ease his suffering and speed recovery. You know he barely survived. He still has a 'crick' in his tail."

Loy, The Elder, had ended the tale with a shake of his head, no doubt remembering the retribution Ahrim later had rendered upon his cowardly demon and goblin allies.

Although not fully recovered, Ahrim was a devilish ally strongly needed by Moloch. Ahrim was an excellent technician, brilliant in improvising and merciless to the weak. His disastrous confrontation with the Archangel Gabriel added to his infamy, but more for its foolhardiness than anything else.

Moloch was happy to let any of that reputation rub off on him and aid his effort to steal the Man's soul.

XIII

Moloch had explained to Ahrim the need for a storm while the Man was at the cemetery for the burial of the Woman's body.

Ahrim figured out the details and executed his initial plan while Moloch was in Denver. He caused confusion at the funeral home to delay the burial three extra days in order to have time for other necessary tasks. He found a good plot of farmland and induced the farmer to harrow it early. The turned over earth would provide better warming of the ground for the thermal updraft they needed.

Ahrim was careful never to use the same trick twice when arranging devilish events. If conditions dictated though, he had no problem abandoning his preferred cruel and monstrous actions to break men and women. For reaping souls he could easily shift gears to sly and cunning techniques of persuasion. Ahrim reveled in manipulating humans into taking apparently innocent actions which in reality had surprisingly pernicious results ensuring the success of his own evil ends. Like all demons, Ahrim would do whatever it took to steal souls.

Ahrim had decided only two areas were necessary for building the thunderstorms needed in Moloch's plan. Later, sitting on the water tower while trying to select a second area, he heard a train whistle to the west. He had explained it all to Moloch. The preferred sites to start the thunderstorms were to the west because of the jet stream and the southwesterly flow from the Baja Gulf. It would be easier to move the storms to the east and northeast. Also, if kept close enough in the beginning, they might be able to move the two storms together for a really frightening display of thunder and lightning.

Ahrim found the train track. Next to it was a large field of corn stalks browning from the midsummer drought. "Hmmm...A hotbox and tumbleweed will do it. And, I'll break the farmer's tractor so he can't cut the cornstalks to make silage." Ahrim's preference was to make the farmer sick, but he didn't have time and there were more important things at stake. Based on Moloch's tale about earlier efforts to steal the Man's soul, Ahrim was sure a confrontation with the angels was inevitable. Although not fully recovered from his bout with Gabriel, he wanted revenge--against any angel, the sooner the better. Ahrim caused swirling winds to move tumbleweed down the railroad tracks and bunch up on the fence between the rails and the cornfield.

On the morning of the funeral Ahrim went back to the railroad tracks and waited. As the 8:10 AM coal train rolled by, he blew on the wheel trucks of the sixty-sixth car. This caused a "hotbox"--overheating in the wheel assembly and brakes. Sparks from the hotbox started the fenced tumbleweed burning and soon the corn was burning. Ahrim rounded up a few goblins to help with the wind necessary to spread the fire just right. That was the smoke seen by Moloch and the other two demons with him.

The Farmhand was almost in a panic. He was on his way to the gas station when he saw the smoke. It was a cornfield he had planted that spring. He had no concern for the corn since only the stalks were left for silage. He was very concerned, however, about that shed in the northeast corner of the field. It had his stash. He had to get to that shed and empty it before it burned. He had to do it before the firemen arrived—or the sheriff. Did he have enough gas to get to the shed and then to the gas station? Doubtful, but the Farmhand knew he had to try. He made a quick U-turn in the old Ford to get back to the shed and his stash. Going too fast, he ran off the road and got stuck. Rocking and rolling the truck forward and back, he finally got it going again with a few choice and unprintable words.

As the field burned, warm air rose into the sky. Gradually the rising smoke was capped with a small, dirty white and puffy cloud. Moisture already in the air from the southwest flow coming from far away in the Baja Gulf condensed as it rose into the cooler air. The condensing moisture turned into cloud. The fire warmed the earth considerably and the heat kept rising. A light wind allowed the small cumulus cloud to build and strengthen. A thunderstorm was being born. Diversion. That's what Ahrim wanted next.

The Farmhand could just envision the problems if the fire reached that shed before he had a chance to empty it. He would just keep driving until he passed out of state—maybe several states. He had a million Quaalude tablets, a little cocaine and a kilo of heroin in that shed. He was really out on a limb as he still owed money for most of it, but the opportunity for a killing—even in small Memphis--was too much to pass up. He was in debt to some very mean people. He worried that now maybe it could end up being the wrong kind of "killing."

Then the Farmhand laughed to himself: "I need to lighten up. It is so easy to get those school kids involved. Pick one or two of the older ones and they will recruit younger ones to support their own habit. Give them a little heroin almost free at first, and the rest—as they say—is easy."

And it was easy. The kids thought they could experiment with one or two doses and then drop the drugs, but not so, especially with heroin. The Farmhand believed he was on the road to easy street; he was the Pied Piper of Memphis

The wind shifted from goblin interference, and the fire moved away from the shed. The Farmhand made it to the shed without being seen by the firemen working the west edge of the fire. He had the shed emptied, the old truck loaded and he was on his way again to the gas station when he passed the sheriff going the other way.

Ahrim was intent upon finding something to keep the angels focused on anything other than Moloch and his crew. Ahrim moved over the route between the funeral home and cemetery. “Ahah,” he observed, “there, a gas station at the crossroads.”

"You goblins get out of that fire and come along," he called.

"But the firemen, can't we bedevil the firemen?" they asked in a chorus.

"You act like ogres! You'll get your chance. NOW OUT! Get yourselves to that gas station," pointing.

Ahrim's tone and brimstone breathe left little doubt about the threat of his impatience. The goblins kept running into each other all the way to the gas station to be the first there and the first to comply with the angry demon's command.

Ahrim cased the area when he reached the station. His plan would work. He just needed a human creature to come by—one that he could use to make his plan a reality. Ahrim sat on a gas pump and waited. Several cars and trucks drove up for gas. Ahrim made sure each human that used the gas pump had trouble with the automatic cutoff lever on the pump nozzle. Soon it was bent enough that it would stick to the 'on' position unless forcibly turned off.

The procession was leaving the funeral home 30 minutes away when Ahrim found his mark. An old Ford farm truck had driven up to the gas pump stopping with a screech. Ahrim quickly saw the darkened soul in the front of the truck and the illegal drugs in the back of the truck.

The driver threw a cigarette out the window of the old truck as he pulled up to the gas pump in an abrupt stop. He had a cigarette pack in hand as he slid out of the truck and reached for the gas hose.

Yes, there it was--between the first and second fingers--tobacco stain. "Oh, this is going to be fun," murmured the demon. That tobacco stain meant a heavy user. The Farmhand certainly wouldn't go for a long time without a drag on a cigarette.

"Perfect," thought Ahrim, "this one surely will do." But then Ahrim had misgivings. Here was a human, who if left alone, would cause many souls to be damaged, and those damaged souls would be perfect prey for the Satan's minions in the future. Although suddenly reluctant, Ahrim knew he had to concentrate on the most important mission of that moment—Moloch's quest to gain the Man's soul. It was turning into a major confrontation with all of Tartarus and Heaven beginning to mobilize for the conflict. Ahrim was not going to be found wanting in doing his part.

Ahrim shook off his reluctance and smiled. He whispered in the Farmhand's ear and exhaled brimstone fumes in his face. This was the perfect prescription for inducing nicotine craving. It took little effort by Ahrim to get the worker to pull matches from his pocket. The Farmhand turned on the gas pump and set the automatic dispenser latch on the nozzle while he simultaneously opened the cigarette box. He walked away from the gas pump to light a cigarette. His moving away gave Ahrim a momentary start. But then after discarding the burnt match and taking two puffs on the cigarette, the Farmhand returned to the side of the truck and the gas hose. With the burning cigarette hanging from his lips, he waited for the gas tank to fill.

As soon as Ahrim was certain the Farmhand would stay there, he spun up a dust devil. "I like the name 'dust devil'," Ahrim thought, "so appropriate." The whirlwind hit. It staggered and blinded the Farmhand. He bumped into the gas nozzle knocking it to the ground. The broken cut-off feature did not work, and gas poured over the ground. The Farmhand slipped. He and the cigarette fell in the growing puddle of gasoline.

Whoosh...whoosh........WHOOMB! First the gas, then the truck burst into flames. The truck was burning only a few seconds before its gas tank exploded. Ahrim knew the gas station would be a ball of flame in ten minutes. He policed up the soul of the dead Farmhand, took a bite and packed the rest away for his gift tribute to the Satan. He then took an extra second to bask in the middle of the fire chortling, "Yes, angels, we have a nice warm fire for you."

Ahrim called to the four goblins, "Sit in this fire and do not leave, even if it is put out. The angels must find you here."

The goblins liked the idea of the new fire and the renewed chance to tease and harass the firefighters, but the thought of angels was not pleasant. "Where will you be?" asked one.

"No matter," was the reply. Ahrim wasn't about to tell those goblins anything. They were expendable and he didn't want them giving out any information to save themselves in a confrontation with the angels. "You just stay here until I come back," he warned.

Ahrim's next stop was the field recently harrowed. The farmer, induced by Ahrim's subconscious urging, had finished his fall harrowing of two fields the day before. The sun was warming the overturned earth more than the surrounding fields. Already a thermal updraft of air was rising. Very soon it would be creating another cumulus cloud that could be used by the demons to produce thunder and lightning essential for their plan.

"Whatcha doin'?"

"You slimy goblin, following me? Get back to the fire like I told you," screamed Ahrim.

Turning to vent his wrath on the wayward goblin, Ahrim saw not what he expected. There radiating in all his own glory was an angel--and it hurt. Ahrim flinched.

George 6234 had seen Ahrim over the field and hurried over to see what deviltry was afoot. The evil demon was so immersed in thought about something nearby--George 6234 couldn't see what--that the angel was able to move next to him before speaking in a voice that mimicked a goblin.

"What fire?" asked George 6234.

Ahrim raged, "Away, away, spirit! You tread dangerously!"

The demon Ahrim, remembering his humbling experience with Gabriel, was all the more enraged that this novice had snuck up on him--had tricked him with a goblin voice. Ahrim flicked his long tongue, his tail and his tongue again. He tried to circle the angel and then made a slight, threatening move.

"My, my," commented George 6234. That and a beatific smile were the only response to the threatening demon.

Ahrim pulled up short. No, no...plenty of time for that he thought. An engagement now could spoil everything. Displaying unusual patience for a demon, Ahrim disengaged and was gone.

This mild behavior, unusual for a demon, was not lost upon George 6234. "Something is definitely afoot," mused George 6234, "and it is not going to be good. Fun maybe, but not good."

SPREADING THE FIRE

XIV

The angels were monitoring the funeral procession which had just started when the town fire siren went off for the third time that day. Ever expectant of a confrontation with the demons over the Man's soul, the angels were wary about any unusual event like a fire siren.

George 6234 had reported on his investigation of the fire that morning along the railroad tracks.

It appeared innocent enough. It was away from the town, the cemetery and the route in-between. Yes, it appeared innocent enough...until the presence of Ahrim was factored in.

"Cristobal, I see no evidence it was caused by demons," reported George 6234. "But, Ahrim did mention fire when he mistook me for a goblin."

"Any demons or ogres around the field on fire?" the other angel asked.

"No. No goblins or witches either."

"How about the firefighters? Are they having any trouble?"

"No," replied George 6234. "I looked at that. Their equipment is operating well. They have a Small Lake nearby which is providing plenty of water, but they decided to let the fire burn out. The farmer was going to burn it anyway, so the firemen left one small unit there to monitor."

"A diversion maybe?" asked Cristobal.

"An unusual one if it is," responded George 6234. The fire burning the field actually is benefiting the farmer. That would be unusual if it were demons' work."

Ahrim had been successful in making the fire in the corn field appear to be a coincidence. Only later would the angels realize its significance.

The angels continued their watch as the funeral procession moved on through town. Cristobal was with the first car where the Cousin and the Man rode behind the hearse. Mercy 1021 made sure the Friend was in the last car so he could cover the rear of the cavalcade. George 6234 roamed as he had no assignment until the Woman's spirit joined them at the cemetery for the graveside service.

George 6234 had felt the new siren before he heard it. He rose and immediately called to Cristobal upon seeing the smoke.

"It is a fire at the crossroads on the route to the cemetery," he reported. "It must have been burning even as I was talking to Ahrim. I guess I was diverted by the fire at the railroad tracks...still I don't know how I missed this new one."

"This one is not a coincidence. It must be the fire that Ahrim mentioned," said Cristobal.

"I tend to agree, but why start the fire so soon before we are to pass the crossroads and the fire?" asked George 6234.

Cristobal, realizing that George 6234 was new in this guardian angel game offered some friendly instruction.

"Remember, our logic is not demons' logic. Demons are very devious. They like diversions--as much for the suffering they cause to bystanders as for the help the diversion gives to their main objective. I've seen them create diversions when they weren't really necessary or were so obvious as to be useless. Wanton destruction is just part of their nature. There are times when I am sure that 'destructive diversion' is an unalterable rule in the Devil's text on warfare."

"When there is a possibility a demon has created havoc, think of Chess. (Angels love chess.) Look at all the possibilities. As you have seen, goblins are easier to understand," he continued. "Goblins generally are pretty straight forward in the problems they create. They can be imaginative and sometimes even plan ahead but seldom are they devious. Ogres are just out for trouble. If you encounter goblins or ogres, always check to see if a demon is around. Witches are a wild card; they like to operate alone. Some are smart and some are not so smart."

"Well we know demons are in on this," said George 6234.

"Yes, for sure. Go check on that fire. We need to keep Cornelius informed," advised Cristobal. "Mercy 1021 and I will stay with the funeral procession."

George was immediately at the gas station--or what used to be a gas station. He saw the four goblins cavorting in the fire. As the goblins became aware of his presence they moved to the very heart of the fire and the exploding gas tanks. As George came closer they became agitated but did not leave.

"Vermin, what evil is this?" asked George 6234.

The goblins at first appeared ready to flee but then huddled together. Finally one stood up as if to confront the angel. Rather than move toward George 6234, he stood to the side less than an arm's length from the other three. No reply was offered.

"Well?"

"We were just having fun," croaked a goblin who spouted water at the flames.

"You're a water gargoyle. Are you playing with fire? And, why are you here?"

"Her idea--my cousin," said the water gargoyle, pointing to one of the three goblins. Goblins normally didn't stay around when confronted by angels. These three plus the one George 6234 now recognized as a lost gargoyle may have felt safety in numbers, but George 6234 doubted that. Blaming each other was typical and of no consequence. George 6234 was sure a demon was involved, but which demon? Of course Ahrim had mentioned fire when George 6234 had surprised him. But George 6234 also knew that Asmodeus was around, although at the cemetery when last seen. Still, Asmodeus had a reputation for using fire in his evil deeds. He wondered if this were the work of Asmodeus, or had Moloch enlisted even another ally? Rumor on the circuit was that Temptation 16 had left Denver with Moloch. Yet it was Ahrim who was the closest in time and space, and the one who mentioned fire. George 6234 remembered Operating Rule Number 23: take nothing for granted.

"This is demon's work. Who?" George 6234 demanded of the goblins.

"Ahrim. That's who. We are under his protection. You leave us alone!" The lead goblin was trying to look defiant while at the same time cowering in fear.

It was more of a wail than a threat. George 6234 hovered and thought. Ahrim! The three little goblins and one out of place gargoyle suddenly became of little consequence. Ahrim had mentioned a fire; it must have been this one. To what end? That question was another matter---a very serious matter. And what about the other fire? Coincidence? Diversion? A key element?

"Leave the firemen alone," commanded George 6234 as he flew off.

"Cristobal, Ahrim set the fire at the crossroads. He's in with Moloch and Asmodeus," advised George 6234.

"Find Cornelius and tell him we have a new player. Return quickly," answered Cristobal.

"Mercy 1021," called Cristobal, "Ahrim is in the thick of it."

"I count four powerful demons," replied Mercy 1021. "Do you suppose there are any more?"

XV

Meanwhile, the morning of the funeral, Cornelius had been checking out the weather. He'd already spent the previous night watching the weather channel. Using the United States Weather Service just made it all a little easier--a nice crosscheck for his own weather forecasting...and weather making. He concurred with the charting of highs and lows and the placement of the jet stream. He thought the Weather Service was a little optimistic about the stability of the Bermuda High over the southeastern United States, and so had sent half of the legion of angels given by Archangel Gabriel to reinforce the high pressure area and keep it from moving out to the east. Cornelius needed the high to stay in place. The Bermuda High was almost a guarantee of clear weather. If the High moved from the southeastern portion of the United States to the east over the Atlantic Ocean, then weather clouds could move over Texas. Cornelius' plan did not include clouds over Texas.

Cornelius was in the stratosphere rechecking the position of high and low pressure areas. They seemed to be holding their forecast position and their influence on the jet stream was as expected. Cornelius put the other half of his legion of angels along the jet stream. The jet stream was essential to the success of his plan. Fortunately it also was easily influenced, given sufficient prior planning and forces. The angels were there for two reasons: first, to move the jet stream if necessary; second, to stop any dark influences from interfering with Cornelius' plan

"Ahh, Cornelius, here you are," greeted George 6234.

"Anybody following you?" asked Cornelius.

"No." George 6234 knew "anybody" meant demons, goblins, ogres or witches.

"And?"

"Ahrim is in it," said George 6234.

"We are in for a bit a trouble then," said Cornelius. "Moloch made a lucky choice--or did he know what we were planning? No, I think he just got lucky."

"Why do you say that?"

"Ahrim has a history of using weather to help in his insidious deeds. We will have to work extra hard to insure our weather plan is not put in jeopardy by Ahrim's presence."

"We have also confirmed the presence of Asmodeus and an uncommon number of demons."

"Yes, I thought I had seen Asmodeus earlier. Temptation 16 is in it too. That's at least four demons. Go to Saint Agnes. She is in Los Angeles. Tell her I need the reserve legion of angels just for today. Tell her, she is invited if she thinks man's "city of angels" can afford to be without her for awhile. I think maybe we will have a battle on our hands."

George 6234 was quickly on his way and had no trouble finding St. Agnes.

"St. Agnes, Cornelius sends his regards," greeted George 6234. "Are you...ah...aware of the situation he has?"

"Yes," was the reply. "It must be getting worse. Otherwise you would not be here. Do you need my reserve legion of angels?"

George 6234 nodded. The St. Agnes Angel Legion was an expanded legion, almost twice the size of most other Angel Legions. It would be a strong reserve force.

"They are yours. What is the opposition?"

"We thank you. Moloch. Asmodeus, Temptation 16 and Ahrim are there--and we think two, large phalanxes of demons, many goblins, some misplaced gargoyles and of course--ogres. Cornelius also extended an invitation to you if you can spare the time."

"The offer is appreciated, but Los Angeles is just too bloody. The people can do without the legion for awhile, but I personally need to keep track of some of the community leaders who have allowed evil to harden their hearts. It is worse here than ancient Rome. Still, if your situation gets desperate, give me a call. For now, Pliny, my number two, will be in command."

George 6234 and Pliny, now the acting commander of the St. Agnes Angel Legion, found Cornelius over the Grand Canyon.

"Pliny, you look robust. You obviously are well recovered from your last foray against the demons," greeted Cornelius.

Pliny was robust, larger than the average angel. His aura was bright and his wings were full. As operations officer of the St. Agnes Legion of Angels he had experienced much contact with The Satan's phalanxes of demons.

The "last foray" mentioned by Cornelius referred to the oil fires of Kuwait. "Foray" understated the size and intensity of the battle between angel and demon forces. Lucifer had induced the Iraqi army to set the Kuwaiti and some Iraqi oil fields on fire. He then overloaded the area with demons in an attempt to keep the oil fires burning. The demons were so ensconced in the burning area that the smoke appeared a fortress. The St. Agnes Legion had been sent in as shock troops to breach the demons' circle of defense. The Legion's "Concentration of Force," an acknowledged principle of war, strangely caught the demons by surprise. The demons fought back with normal ferocity but unusual tenacity and a stalemate ensued.

The demons felt like they were fighting for Gehenna and Tartarus. The magnitude of fire and smoke resembled hell. It was as if the angels had invaded their home.

Gabriel had committed two legions of angels against a larger force of demon phalanxes, goblin skulks and ogre skirmishers. The St. Agnes Legion had maintained contact with the demons for a full month with angels scorched and even burned in places by the brimstone. Finally Pliny led a special unit on a flanking movement to out-maneuver the demon forces and break the stalemate. The bold stroke won the day for the forces of good. Although wounded and faded Pliny's aura had maintained sufficient strength to be quickly rejuvenated by the grace of prayers from around the world.

"I understand you have some real nasties cornered, Cornelius," laughed Pliny. More seriously, "Will it be a battle?"

"I'm almost certain," replied Cornelius. He then told the whole story to Pliny. "I believe Moloch has too much at stake to quit now. He seems to have put his reputation on the line. And, the presence of three other major demons bodes ill. The Satan apparently is backing Moloch with unusual support. I suspect The Satan senses an opportunity to breach the Plan."

Lucifer, The Satan, wanted chaos. Jehovah God forbade chaos. God's Plan had to be upheld despite constant attacks upon it by Lucifer. Lucifer, a fallen angel--a fallen archangel--hated Jehovah God, hated the angels who remained with him and hated man made in God's image. Lucifer was intent upon destroying the Plan and thus destroying all. He had enough successes against humankind and near successes against the Plan that he never lost his appetite for evil and warfare.

"Pliny, hold the St. Agnes Legion in reserve," said Cornelius. "Be ready at a moment's notice. Stay within hailing distance."

"But not noticeable, I assume," replied Pliny.

"Good point," said Cornelius. "You are correct. We really don't want the demons to know how seriously we are taking this. They are already wary of the many guardian angels we have in the funeral party. If they see a legion of angels on hold, they will bring up more reinforcements. But, more important, I want the element of surprise. I'm sure they won't suspect the involvement of the angel legion we have monitoring the Bermuda High. They are too far east--and downwind."

"How about Colorado Springs?"

"Colorado Springs? Yes, it is close enough, but...."

Pliny held up his hand. "We'll take an outing to the Air Force Academy Chapel. It's pretty and the younger angels like sliding up and down the spires. We'll make it look like a holiday. The demons couldn't suspect, even if one passes by."

"I like it. It will strengthen you for any battle should the demons decide to engage."

"Yes, despite its name, man's 'City of Angels' can be wearing. My legion can use the break and renewal."

"Done," said Cornelius, "await my call."

ANGELS TAKE HOLIDAY AT AIR FORCE ACADEMY CHAPEL

XVI

On their way back to Memphis, Texas, Cornelius had a thought. "George 6234," he said, "let's have another look at the cemetery. I doubt that anything has changed. The demons would not be foolish enough to tip their hand so early, but you never can tell. I'm certain the gas station fire at the crossroads is a diversion, but then that leaves in question the fire by the railroad tracks."

"I saw demons and goblins at the gas station fire, but none at the corn field by the railroad tracks. Do you think that one is a diversion too?" asked George 6234.

"No...I think not. Double diversions are not a normal demon practice. Nor do I think it is an accident. I am not willing to accept that coincidence. Yet, I don't see what it accomplishes."

"It actually benefits the farmer too," reminded George 6234.

Over Memphis on their way to the cemetery, George 6234 asked Cornelius, "Is this a good idea? Are we not showing too much interest?"

"We are just going to look. You are right that we must be careful and not alarm Moloch and the others. I have two objectives. Most important, I need to double-check the layout. Secondly, I want to disturb those goblins Moloch sent there. The more fearful they are of us, the less trouble they can cause the Man and the others in the funeral party."

"What about the layout?" asked George.

"Well, there is the parking, the grave, the seats and the awning. The seats need to face approximately southwest into the afternoon sun. It would be best if there were no awning, but if there is, then it can't be too low. The parking should be behind the seats. There should be little room to stand on the west side of the grave site."

"There certainly are a bunch of the little nasty things down there," said George 6234, referring to the many goblins and ogres lounging on the graves as he and Cornelius arrived at the cemetery.

"Ruffle their feathers will you," tasked Cornelius. "Gently at first, I may need more commotion later."

Smiling, George 6234 moved to confront the evil spirits. His smile was as unnerving to the cowardly goblins as anything he could have done. George first feinted action in one direction and then another. He then circled the goblins and ogres causing them even more concern.

George 6234 menaced the goblins who responded by moving among the tombstones squawking. Cornelius observed the arrangements around the grave site. It was almost perfect for his needs. Chairs and canopy aligned just right. Parking was naturally to the east as was a standing area for those who could not find a chair in which to sit.

"George," Cornelius said in a low voice as the other angel passed close. "See if you can cause a little more disturbance, and get the leaves off the south side of that tree," pointing.

"Carte blanche?" asked the other.

"Carte blanche," replied Cornelius.

Fifty goblins were no match for George 6234. His sudden increase in energy caught them unaware. George 6234 ran, charged, and bent low and swooped. It was like a bowling ball run amok. The goblins and ogres, ordered to stay at the cemetery by Asmodeus and Moloch, were running into tombstones in their effort to avoid the fast moving angel. Cornelius watched in amusement as two goblins made the mistake of trying to hide on top of the same monument at the same time. The result was a small thunderclap. George 6234 then decided it was time to take the leaves off the side of the tall oak tree as Cornelius had asked. Unfortunately for them, six ogres took up hiding in the tree just before George arrived in a golden whirlwind.

A small earthquake was registered in northwest Texas that morning. It was followed by heavy dark storm clouds that generated funnels and tornados.

With rapidly fading concern for the wrath of Moloch and Asmodeus, the remaining goblins were helter skelter and then gone. Their fear of the rampaging angel was now! They would worry about the two demons later. The more defiant left with a gnashing of teeth, but it was only show. A few witches watched from afar and never challenged the angels.

"Well done, George 6234," congratulated Cornelius. "We just might make you a warrior angel instead of a guardian angel."

"It was fun," said George 6234, "much better than tackling Moloch."

"And I enjoyed watching," said Cornelius.

"Are we rid of them?"

"About half of the goblins will come back. Still the demons will not be happy with a fifty percent reduction in their forces. I don't think the witches will engage unless driven by the demons."

"Do we need to do anything else now?" asked George 6234.

"All is well here until the Man arrives for the graveside service. Let's go join Cristobal and the funeral procession."

XVII

Moloch, Asmodeus, Temptation 16 and Ahrim were conferring in their favorite, Memphis sewer with green ooze on the floor and black slime on the walls. Ahrim was sitting on a dead rat. The stench would have been unbearable even without the presence of the demons. They had just started planning the final destruction of the Man when suddenly Loki appeared.

"Lucifer sends his luck," greeted Loki.

"And a spy," growled Ahrim.

"Brother, you misjudge me," pleaded the blond demon. "Perhaps your problem is fear or...."

"Enough," growled Asmodeus. "Can't you keep control, Moloch?"

"Are you here to help, Loki, or...?" needled Ahrim some more.

Moloch, needing to establish his leadership, stood up and asked, "Why are you here, Loki?"

"Lucifer sent me to assist. I have available a skulk of goblins and my own phalanx of demons on call."

"Good news at last," shouted Temptation 16.

"What's he know that we don't know?" asked Ahrim.

"Do not question the wisdom of The Dragon," cautioned Asmodeus.

"Irregardless, we can use them," said Moloch, trying to establish control.

"You mean 'regardless'," tittered Ahrim who quickly, but nervously, wanted to divert attention away from his previous, impolitic reference to Lucifer.

The sewer was warming up and Moloch was the source of the heat. He did not need these pip-squeak demons. This stupid rivalry (which Moloch normally enjoyed) was going to ruin everything. These idiots would keep him from winning the Man's soul.

"Ahrim, you are so much ant-dung. Be gone!" he thundered.

Ahrim turned crimson and bared his dripping fangs. One step forward and then Asmodeus put a restraining claw on his upper limb.

"Hold, Ahrim. Outside." Asmodeus led Ahrim to the top of the sewer.

Asmodeus had a vague, bad feeling that convinced him they had to continue and it was best to have Moloch in charge in case of failure. By sending Loki, Lucifer was showing an unusual, but direct interest in the battle for the Man's soul. Lucifer encouraged competition among his fallen angels—his demons--but drew the line when it interfered with his own personal war against Jehovah and the men made in Jehovah's image.

"We are in this too deep," cautioned Asmodeus. "Lucifer is aware and has sent help. That means he has great interest. If this fails for bickering, Moloch will point the finger. You and I will suffer The Dragon's wrath, not Moloch."

A grudging agreement from Ahrim and both demons returned to the foul sewer which was reminiscent of home.

"Well? If you are not with me in this, then you are not necessary. The Man's soul must be ours. If you would not win a sorry soul for Lucifer, then leave. If you do not care, then leave. If you have no interest in the Final Battle, then leave."

Moloch's words were crisp, bitter--and calculated. The others had no recourse but to stay and cooperate--with Moloch in charge.

"Are we five?" asked Moloch.

Each of the other demons--Asmodeus, Ahrim, Temptation 16 and Loki—nodded agreement.

"Good," said Moloch. "Thanks to Ahrim, our storm clouds are building. Ahrim, when we are done here take Loki's phalanx of demons and work the clouds. Don't go directly there, but take a circuitous route in case you are seen by the angels with the funeral procession. Build those clouds, but also protect them. We cannot let the angels disperse the clouds. We need rain, thunder and lightning.

"Loki, you back up Ahrim with half your goblins, but stay in the shadows. I don't think the angels know you are here. Your presence could be a shock they will find difficult to counter."

"Temptation 16, go to Tartarus and Gehenna. Get several skulks of ogres to sit in the clouds. Their static energy will help the demons and increase the blue lightning. You might stop by Yugoslavia and pick up any spare witches--a couple of covens if you can get them. We'll need them to help the demons with the clouds."

Moloch stopped and thought. This was all going too quickly. He slowly turned around several times surveying the scene—surveying his "battlefield." This was war! He thought back to ancient battles. He remembered Clausewitz. Then Moloch realized he was scattering his limited forces, and that was not good—er, not wise.

"Temptation 16,' he called, "we also require more demons. Ask Lucifer for two phalanxes of demons. Tell him they will be reserves for Loki." The reference to Loki should speed that request; Moloch smiled at his own cleverness.

A major battle was developing in this long standing war between good and evil. Moloch would need those extra demons.

"Asmodeus, I will give to you the other half of the skulk of goblins that Loki brought. Use them with those I left at the cemetery this morning to keep the guardian angels and the Christians off balance. You are my diversion while I concentrate on the Man. And keep that George 6234 away from me if he is there."

Moloch had been hurt by the contact with George 6234 much more than the angels had realized. Moloch knew he was no match in a one-on-one with the new, young and exceptionally strong angel.

"Do you really need almost a whole skulk of goblins at the cemetery? That's a lot of goblins," said Temptation 16.

"Yes it is, but I'm not sure how many angels to expect at the cemetery," replied Moloch. "Many of the friends of the Woman are strong Christians. I want half a skulk of goblins just for them alone. The cemetery is the key. The Man will be at his lowest then. It is the best chance...no, opportunity...to steal his soul. I want you, Temptation 16, to be there as well...after you drop off the ogres and witches in the storm clouds."

XVIII

The fire at the cross roads was still burning as the funeral procession passed. The volunteer fire departments from Memphis and Hedley had it under control. Despite the earlier warning from George 6234, the four goblins left at the gas station fire by Ahrim still couldn't resist bedeviling the firemen, but their black hearts weren't in it. George 6234 had scared them. As the funeral procession passed with its coterie of guardian angels, the goblins completely lost heart and fled. They wanted to be as far away as possible from the angels--and from Ahrim who they were disobeying.

Cornelius and George 6234 met the funeral procession as it passed the crossroads and the burning gas station. The absence of demons there and the fleeing goblins verified that it had been a diversion as the angels suspected.

"Cristobal, anything?" asked Cornelius.

"Just this fire," was the reply. "Looks like a diversion."

"I agree. I am sure Moloch has something planned at the cemetery. It can get a little crowded there if four major demons are going to be involved. It may be just as simple as a head-on, brute force attack. Or it may be something more devious. I have Pliny and the St. Agnes Legion standing by."

"Anything special you want me to do?" asked Cristobal.

"The Man is the target. But the demons will be after maximum mayhem. They'll hurt anything they can."

"Four demons certainly mean more than a few goblins, too."

"Yes, and witches and ogres."

"Besides me and Mercy 1021 there are four other guardian angels," said Cristobal. "The Woman's friends are a strong Christian group."

"Good, you and the other guardian angels watch the Christians and all the other men. I expect the Cousin and Friend will stay close to the Man. They will require special surveillance as the demons will be concentrated around the Man. The goblins and ogres can cause just enough confusion and distractions to make it very dangerous. It will help if you keep the Christians and their guardian angels spread out in a circle around the Man. The goblins will hesitate to enter the circle. And the demons will be busy trying to control their forces."

"Are we to watch the Man also?"

Cornelius thought a moment and then replied, "George 6234 will take care of the Man. George 6234 also will have the Woman's spirit there with Mercy 1021 available to help protect them both. Cristobal, you will be in charge at the cemetery. George and Mercy 1021 will be enough to protect the Woman's spirit while I'm elsewhere."

"And you, elsewhere? You certainly aren't going to miss the fun?" asked Cristobal.

"I'll be around. Our success will depend on the sign the Man asked for--the Glory. That's my department," answered Cornelius.

"If Moloch figures that out, you will be under full scale attack," advised Cristobal. "You may have set out the most dangerous part for yourself."

"That's why Pliny and his Angel Legion are in reserve. This could be an all out battle, but I have seen no sign of a build-up of forces on the other side."

The procession was moving into the cemetery.

"George 6234, it is time to bring the Woman's spirit; and, be careful," advised Cornelius.

George 6234 returned to the abode of angels to pick up the Woman's spirit.

Gabriel was there. "Cornelius is ready then?" asked Gabriel.

"Yes, he sent me for the Woman's spirit," answered George 6234. "There are four demons and at least two skulks of goblins with an uncounted number of ogres and witches expected."

"There will be five demons. We've had a sighting that Loki, the Blond Demon, is in the area also."

George 6234 had never seen Loki but knew of him by reputation. Loki was an old world spirit of evil--a blond, almost pretty giant, whose beautiful exterior concealed an inner core of unimaginably evil bile. Loki was a favorite of Lucifer and so was given his own personal phalanx of demons. His presence would change the odds considerably. It also meant that Lucifer could have developed a very personal interest in this battle for the Man's soul. The odds were getting worse. How many phalanxes of demons were there?

Gabriel could feel George 6234's increased concern.

"Do not fret," counseled the Archangel. "Just make sure that Cornelius and Cristobal are aware. I have already advised Pliny that his Angel Legion will most assuredly be needed. Now, it is time for you to return with the Woman's spirit."

The Woman's spirit appeared as if by prearranged signal.

"It is time," said Gabriel to her. "This will be your last visit to Earth with the Man. It is important. You will see demons. They want the Man."

"The little green demon...," the Woman's spirit grimaced; she shuddered.

"Do not worry. You are in God's grace; you have been faithful; you have loved your God. Now he shows his love for you. Suddenly, the Woman was given two wings of a great eagle that she might fly safely to the earth. Her aura brightened. Her countenance determined.

"I go with love and grace," she replied. "I understand the Plan and know that Cornelius needs my help with the Man. I do not like that demon, but....!"

"Few do," Gabriel laughed. "You are a child of God, go with his blessing." Gabriel embraced her spirit which then took on an even greater intensity of light.

The Woman's spirit, now stronger, with George 6234 at her side, returned to Memphis and the cemetery. Cornelius met them and marveled at the change in the Woman's spirit.

"Gabriel advises that Loki is involved," said George 6234.

"That means another phalanx of demons is somewhere near," said Cornelius.

That's what Gabriel said, and he has advised Pliny."

"Good. I am sure now that Pliny will be needed. I have noticed some storm clouds building to the southwest. We can't have those. I suspect they are Ahrim's work. I must be off. That there will be a Glory is my concern now. Get Mercy 1021. I want you two and the Woman's spirit to be near the Man. You are in charge of the Man and the Woman's spirit. I expect things will get interesting very soon. Be careful. The smell of brimstone is getting heavy."

XIX

With his warning, Cornelius left to check on the building storm clouds. At the same time a skulk of goblins descended on the cemetery to join those few who had returned after George 6234's attack earlier that morning.

The new goblins thought they were out on a lark to harass a small funeral. No one had told them that so many angels would be there.

"One, two...three...four, five angels," exclaimed a goblin.

"No there are six!" screamed another.

"At least twenty!" wailed a third and fourth.

"Are you the Goblins of Satan or silly ogres that you fear only seven angels?" shouted Asmodeus who had just arrived to take charge. "There are demons coming." He flayed the cowering goblins with his tail.

"Keep moving," he told them. "The angels must protect the humans. They will leave the humans and attack you only if you go too slowly. Work in pairs. And,

I want noise! Tear down that canopy. Knock over some chairs. Flatten some tires."

Asmodeus knew if he worked his goblins into a frenzy, they would think less about the intimidating angels, and the ogres would join in just because mayhem was fun.

"Moloch," he called. "I need more goblins. Even witches would help, and where are the extra demons?"

Moloch had also counted seven angels, an unwelcome but not unexpected number. His real problem was that Cornelius was not among them. No matter. He, Moloch would stay near the Man. Yes, there was the Woman's spirit next to the Man. She had strong wings. Moloch hesitated. This was something new. But it was too late now. He started to pounce, but was brought up short as George 6234 and the other angel came into view.

"AHSHEEEORRRRGGGHHH!" Remembering his last encounter with George 6234, Moloch gave a long, snarling groan.

"Careful, little one," warned George 6234. "Do not violate the Rules again."

"I don't know what you are talking about," answered Moloch with a thin, sinister smile on his sharp yellow, shark's teeth. "I am here for the Man. He is mine."

Moloch did not like to be referred to as "little one"--and by an apparently apprentice angel at that. He wanted to put this young, but strangely powerful, angel in his place by some additional and clever remark. He almost missed the next question from George 6234.

George 6234 asked, "The Man is yours?"

"Of course mine. You must be new."

"Oh! Not Lucifer's?" George 6234 smiled broadly.

"Lucifer's! He is Lucifer's!" shouted Moloch.

Why was he letting this overbearing, no account angel bother him wondered Moloch. The presence of Asmodeus did not help. Moloch had that sickening feeling he was not in control--that the angel was up to something.

"And Lucifer BEELZEBUB said you could break the Rules by attacking the Woman's spirit even though she was protected by the Grace of Jehovah God," added George 6234.

As George 6234 had calculated, Asmodeus was distracted from attempting to herd the goblins to his will. Hearing Lucifer called the hated, man-given name "Beelzebub," Asmodeus turned and heard George's 6234 accusation about breaking the Rules.

"Moloch," called a worried Asmodeus.

"We need more help," said a fleeing Moloch. "I will get Temptation 16 and those extra demons you wanted."

Moloch groaned and was gone. He had been keelhauled by a baby, and he didn't like it. Something was wrong. Moloch wondered if there were more forces for good at work in this imbroglio than he had anticipated.

Moloch broke the Rules, wondered Asmodeus. The angel would not lie. No wonder Moloch was so intent upon achieving this victory. Only that could save him if he violated the Rules of the Plan.

As Moloch arrived where the demons were building the storm clouds, Temptation 16 had just delivered ten skulks of ogres and two covens of witches to Ahrim's supervision. Ahrim and the phalanx of demons assigned to him had done a good job building up the storm over the burnt corn field. It was fast becoming a towering cumulonimbus thunderhead, growing darker by the moment with increasing thunder and lightning.

"Temptation 16, good...now put the ogres in the second cloud over that plowed field," called Ahrim.

"Temptation 16, come with me," said Moloch.

"What? Do you want these clouds or not, Moloch?" asked Ahrim.

"I've got seven angels down there," answered Moloch. "I need Temptation 16. Use Loki. The angels know he is here. I'll take the two covens of witches too. They can help the goblins."

"We'll not do goblins' work," said one of the coven leaders.

Moloch attacked with sudden and lethal ferocity. Too late the recalcitrant witch tried to flee, but her fate was determined the instant she spoke.

"Any others," asked the bloody demon.

There was no reply.

"This is serious business. Get yourselves to Asmodeus--Now!"

Moloch was very satisfied. He couldn't have planned it better. The hapless witch, whose dead spirit was now consigned to wail in Sheol forever, had allowed him to instill--at least temporarily--in the remaining witches, and all the goblins and ogres they would tell, a greater fear of the demons than of the angels. And he still had twenty-five witches left to burn. Moloch smiled at his own joke. He would remember to repeat it when he was able finally to boast of his victory in Tartarus.

Moloch looked at Temptation 16. He could see the younger demon was impressed by the decisive and savage action. Hopefully, the seriousness of the hunt would be seen by Loki and Ahrim as well.

"Ahrim," Moloch said "Temptation 16 and I will return to attack the Man and steal his soul. I still need the biggest storm you can make. The sun must not shine. And, be careful, Cornelius has disappeared. I don't know what he plans."

"Loki, take the ogres and slant that other storm over here," directed Ahrim. "I want it to join this one. Then we can build them together. I'll keep your phalanx of demons here to help build this storm cell. Also, once the clouds are joined, we need to move them slightly to the east. After we get the storms high enough, I plan to surround them and protect them with the whole phalanx of demons. We'll keep the ogres in the clouds. They can make hail."

"Have we enough demons?" ask Loki. "That many ogres need more than me to watch them. And, I am starting to feel the presence of many angels. I am itching all over."

Moloch smiled in reply, happy that he had anticipated this. "I sent Temptation 16 to ask Lucifer for two phalanxes of demons to be held in reserve for your command. They should arrive momentarily."

XX

Cornelius was troubled by the storm clouds southwest of the cemetery. They were building much faster than other clouds in the area and they were in the vicinity of the fire that had burned in the corn field that morning. If high enough, the clouds would block out the sun, preventing his fabrication of a Glory. That's it, he realized, the fire...the demons had started the fire to get more thermal heating for cloud build-up. It was exactly the type of deviltry Ahrim was known for.

Cornelius went to the fire site, arriving just as Temptation 16 came with the ten skulks of ogres and two, small covens of witches. Cornelius pulled up and moved sunward where no demon would ever look. There was no danger of him being observed. He watched for a while, seeing the arrival of Moloch and then his departure with Temptation 16 and the two covens of witches. Loki and his phalanx of demons were there just as Gabriel had predicted. Cornelius hurried to Pliny.

"Quick, bring your legion of angels. The demons are building two large thunderstorms that will interfere with the Glory. We must stop them."

"How?" asked Pliny. "We are ready for whatever you need."

"Let's try finesse first," cautioned Cornelius. "We'll use the jet stream. I have an angel legion stationed on it right now. They will lower it and move it to blow the tops off the thunderclouds. We'll dissipate the storm in a very natural fashion. I'll handle that. Your legion will be needed to protect us as we move the jet stream."

"You realize, finesse seldom works with demons," replied Pliny.

"You are right," smiled Cornelius, "but let's start that way. I want you to hold back. If the demons attack, catch them on the flank. Demons are very susceptible to surprise. I prefer a short battle. Remember to listen for our trumpet calls."

Cornelius called together the angels guarding the jet stream and outlined his plan.

"There are at least ten skulks of ogres in the thunderclouds," he warned, "but don't worry about them--and don't let them distract you. The real threat is Loki. He is there with his phalanx of demons and maybe more. Ahrim is there also with several skulks of goblins and ogres. Remember, he is always dangerous...regardless of the odds."

Ahrim and Loki had joined the thunderclouds into one giant storm rising above 60,000 feet when Cornelius and the other angels moved the jet stream against the clouds.

"Loki, do you see them?" shouted Ahrim. "Ten O'clock high! It's a whole legion of angels."

"I've got them. I'm calling my two reserve phalanxes of demons. We'll engage now." The evil forces moved forth as cymbals clashed in a continuous roll of sound.

"I'll bring my goblins and the ogres," said Ahrim. "The clouds are strong enough to stand alone if we can stop the jet stream."

"Not yet," said Loki. "Let the ogres remain. They are doing a good job throwing hail and blue lightning at the people in the cemetery. Remember, Moloch is there to get the Man. The hail and lightning should keep the angels down there busy. Besides, the ogres would just get in the way right now. We may need them after we charge the angels. Do bring the goblins. The goblins are more of a distraction than lethal, but they still will be effective. I do want you to round up the spare demons to follow our charge however. Then be prepared to bring the ogres if I call."

"OK, you're the tactician," said Ahrim. "I know we have at least a skulk of goblins just waiting."

"The angels are scattered out holding the jet stream. Cannon fodder," a guttural laugh from Loki.

The demons' phalanxes formed with an eager Loki in the fore. Sounding like rolls of thunder, their cymbals rang out as each phalanx charged across the sky with Ahrim's howling ogres following on their heels. The angels appeared to be struggling with the jet stream and paid them no heed. A now berserk Loki, caught up in the easy victory, failed to check his left flank.

A trumpet blast. Coming out of the sun, the Saint Agnes Angel Legion caught the charging horde full on the flank. Meanwhile, the trailing demons overran the crush of combatants tumbling headlong into the angels on the jet stream, forcing the angels to turn from their task to ward off the reckless attack.

It was near disaster for the people at the cemetery. Ahrim's thunderstorm burst upon them with little warning. The wind and rain pummeled the funeral party who ran for the cover of the canopy over the chairs. The ogres in the clouds howled with laughter and began throwing large hail and balls of blue lightning to hole the canopy. The witches shook and broke tree branches. Asmodeus and Temptation 16 directed the demons to swirl the winds bringing the wet rain under the flapping tent canopy. The funeral party huddled like shipwrecked sailors under a broken mast and sails. The angels surrounded them, deflecting the lightning and hail. Then Asmodeus sent twenty demons to tear down the tent canopy, himself coming close enough to occupy three of the angels. Temptation 16 worked the other side with the witches as if to complete an encircling maneuver. As the first twenty demons were repulsed, Asmodeus called in forty more.

The guardian angel Franciscus—at the funeral with the Man's squadron mate from long before—was directly at the point of attack. Weakened from the earlier strike, Franciscus fell at the first onslaught of the forty demons but was up quickly. This emboldened the demons and witches who responded by drawing closer with only a little urging by the two senior demons.

Brimstone was in the air. Ozone from the lightning mixed with the sickly stench of the demons. The demons could not quite reach the tent canopy or the people under it, but the evil of their presence was felt by all in the funeral party.

Moloch moved inside the circle of angels to be as close to the Man as possible. Moloch knew he would be OK as long as he did not attempt to strike an angel or touch the Woman's spirit--but he was tempted.

George 6234 and Cristobal kept the Cousin and the Woman's spirit near the Man. George 6234 was careful to insure he was always between Moloch and the Woman's spirit. Mercy 1021, in an effort to keep Moloch off balance, tried to keep always behind him.

The result was a constant movement of angels and demons for position. Seeing the standoff, Temptation 16 withdrew while Asmodeus continued to bait the angels with charging demons. Temptation 16 moved the witches in a complete circle around the funeral party. They appeared as wraiths and ghosts to the fearful people.

Asmodeus was directing demons in twos and threes on high speed suicide attacks across and under the tent canopy. He wanted to heighten the danger to the people and engage the angels even more closely in order to give Moloch a needed opening.

Ahrim held his ogres back and tried to direct his goblins against the main angel force, but the undisciplined goblins preferred the easier and safer target. They went after the people at the funeral tent.

Driven by the frenzy of the storm, the constant cymbals and the battle lust of a long hatred, the demons at first were willing to make foolish attacks. Then as their casualties mounted and numbers dwindled it was harder for Asmodeus to motivate the demons to attack. Soon Asmodeus was forced to lead the demons rather than drive them. Seeing the problem Asmodeus was having with the demons, Temptation 16 managed to scare a few of the witches into direct but futile battle against the defending angels. Both demons were using up their forces fast as they employed hit and run tactics against the angels from the outside while Moloch attempted to sow confusion from the inside.

Only the presence of seven angels kept the funeral party safe and kept Moloch from the Man's soul. The need to protect the people in the funeral party limited the angels to defensive action against the three demons and their force of goblins, ogres and witches.

The storm suddenly lessened and the sky became lighter. Loki and his demons were losing the fight and could not protect the thundercloud.

"Ahrim," cried Loki, "the ogres now." The cymbals signaled another evil charge.

Ahrim joyously led the ogres into the fray. He raged and fought with a fury born of an earlier, remembered defeat. Suddenly he was joined by a new phalanx of demons and a scattering of goblins.

As if hearing and seeing the battle above for the first time, Asmodeus rushed his demons from the cemetery into the bigger fight. He gave Moloch an expectant look as he departed. Moloch knew what was desired and reluctantly ordered Temptation 16 to follow with the witches.

Saint Agnes then arrived. Cornelius was about to send her to bring the legion of angels he had positioned at the Bermuda High, when another loud trumpet blast was heard.

The Archangel Gabriel had already rounded up that legion and was on the scene.

For years after people in the town of Memphis and the counties of Hall and Collingsworth would talk about that day. They remembered the sky was black with heavy clouds. Rain and hail pounded the ground. The sun had disappeared. The only light was from constant lightning bolts that went from cloud to cloud and only a few striking the ground. The thunder sounded like the continuous banging of a thousand cymbals. A few said they had even heard trumpets, but they were laughed at.

XXI

The battle was fully engaged in the plain on the sky. The angels employed the ancient, and not so ancient, formation of "squares" for both offensive and defensive maneuvers. They formed squares of forty to eighty angels. On offense, all angels would face in the direction of movement. On defense, angels on each of the four sides of the square would face out. They were disciplined, synchronized and moved easily as a unit. The forces of the Devil, Lucifer, initially started with the same tactics, but having far less discipline, their formations soon dissolved with demons, goblins and ogres attacking in two's and three's. The demons reduced their effectiveness by ignoring the Principle of Concentration of Forces and Principle of Control. But that was their nature.

Heaven and hell fought over one man's soul. But more than that, Lucifer wanted to destroy the Plan. The Plan was proof that Jehovah God was supreme.

For their part, the angels were intent upon clearing the sky and keeping it clear so Cornelius could again bring forth the Glory as a sign to the Man.

The evil ones, urged on by Ahrim, Loki and Asmodeus wanted to blot out all light.

Suddenly the cymbals grew louder; from nowhere, nine skulks of ogres rushed directly at the angels--a sight seldom seen as ogres almost never confronted angels in any manner regardless of numbers. A mere glance by an angel usually left the weaker ogres with the ability to do nothing but gnash their teeth in helpless fury. This mindless ferocity by the ogres in attacking the angels could only mean that Lucifer, The Dragon, was close by.

Gabriel took notice, but continued to direct the angels with trumpet calls as they worked in silent, synchronized precision, alternately brightening and dimming as the battle flowed. Demon and ogre alike resorted to individual attack and bravado. The goblins preferred to work in pairs. They all brayed, whooped and whistled while slinging fiery darts of brimstone, but to no avail. The forces of evil knew their strange noises often made men fearful and easier to vanquish, but Satan's minions could never accept that angels were immune to devilish noises. Had they taken more care with their brimstone, they would have been much more effective, but that was not the way of demons or goblins, and certainly not ogres.

The angels were advancing, clearing the sky. They grappled and threw the demon forces back. It was a fierce battle with losses on both sides, but the angels' superior discipline and tactics were winning the day. The angels controlled the jet stream. They lowered it and held it against the rising storm clouds.

Suddenly--a giant thunderclap! Earth and heavens reverberated. The battle lulled as combatants stopped in wonder. Cymbals and trumpets fell silent. The main storm cloud grew like the mushroom of a nuclear bomb. The black, dense cloud roiled as a towering inferno. It was weather gone mad. The cloud top was crowned with a hellish red halo of dancing lightning bolts. Thunder was the continuous roar of a thousand freight trains.

Then all was quiet. At the pinnacle was the bloody visage of The Dragon.

Lucifer gestured and roared. He beat his chest, raged and swept aside ally and enemy alike with his mighty tail He reached down to the depths of Sheol picking up a thousand dead souls. He threw them at the now still angels. When his words came in a hollow growl, they still were clear and distinct to each spirit in the battle.

"Who would oppose me?" asked The Satan. "I know you and you...and you," pointing to the angels. "I ask who would oppose me for a little man's soul?"

Lucifer's roiling cloud spread across the sky like a stormy sea. The angels, resolute, held their position, but there was a dimming here and there.

"Hold, hold," shouted Gabriel as he raised his trumpet.

And all was quiet. Then the evil forces started to cheer.

A bolt of lightning crossed the sky, and all was quiet again...nothing but silence, as all waited for what was to come.

A lone trumpet call sounded.

"I AM THAT I AM. I AM WHAT I WOULD BE!!" YAHWEH spoke. It was a voice like many waters, and the heavens were torn open.

And another voice was raised, "These will wage war against the Lamb, and the Lamb will overcome them, because He is Lord of lords and King of kings. Those who are with Him are the called and chosen and faithful."

The jet stream doubled in size and strength. It was as if a mighty river flowed across the sky. Lucifer's cloudy seat could not stand before the power. It broke and scattered—like it had never been. Lucifer recoiled and then leaned forward as if to attack. He raged at the onslaught of God's goodness and Grace. Lucifer lunged right, then left, but was driven back...back... back....

Buffeted and battered, a wounded Lucifer fell and fell, screeching and mewling. He tumbled twice and then was gone.

Until the Day of Judgment, Lucifer, The Dragon, would continue his war against Jehovah God and those made in God's image, but he would not again leave the hellish sanctuary of Tartarus until after he had a long rest--and after he settled with Moloch for (unsuccessfully) breaking the Rules of the Plan.

With the swift defeat of Lucifer, demon, goblin, ogre and witch alike fled, making no sound but saving all their strength for flight. Only silent, shining angels remained in a clear, glorious sky.

Then came a spontaneous chorus: "Alleluia, Alleluia, Al-le-lu-ia…."

XXII

Now was the time. Cornelius moved. He rechecked his line of sight between the Man and the sun. Ah, there. That polished tombstone would work. He moved again, turning just so. The sun's light was magnified and reflected.

"As we remember our sister and her devotion ...," the minister was finishing a long graveside oration that had been often interrupted by wind, rain, hail and lightning.

Despite Lucifer's defeat and the immediate departure thereafter of all the other demons, Moloch had still remained near the Man. All hope was lost, but his very existence was in jeopardy. He could not leave without doing something.

The Man, in his sorrow, had heard nothing. He had forgotten everything except his loss. He saw nothing, he felt nothing but loneliness. His deep misery blocked out the presence of the Woman's spirit. George 6234 could see that some action was necessary. As Cornelius moved in the sky, George 6234 brushed against the Man. Startled by the silent and invisible touch, the Man looked up.

A dazzling sunbeam reflected off the tombstone to his right. It transfixed the Man and held him in its aura.

The appearance of the Glory had also momentarily frozen Moloch who remembered its pain last time he touched it. Now with a scream he moved as if to intercede

"It's too late, Moloch," said George 6234.

Moloch stopped, flickered and then was gone in a small puff to suffer his ignominious fate.

To the Woman's spirit, George 6234 said, "Move into the sunbeam."

"As you wish," came her doubting reply. She moved and became part of the Glory.

"Is it you?" the Man asked.

"By the Grace of God, I am with you," she answered.

"But...?" The Man had asked for a sign but still did not understand.

"Do you remember our pact?" She asked.

The Man had a bewildered look on his face. "Hmmm," was all he could reply.

"We agreed," she said, "if despite my fear, I would fly with you in your biplane, then you despite your misgivings would go to church with me. We did it—several times. Did we not both survive; did we not both actually have fun? You know we did, and you were surprised and pleased – very pleased. See now, I fly with no problem. It is a gift from God." She gave one stroke of her new wings; rose two feet off the ground and settled gently back down.

"But…," the Man replied.

"No, buts." The voice was firm but loving. "I am here. Jehovah God sent me. The Spirit is here. We are here for you. We love you. Can you not love us?"

"You know I loved you....No, I love you now."

"And trust me?" she pressed.

"Of course," he replied.

"But not my God, who brought me here--Jehovah who honored you with the gift of the second sign you asked for--the Glory?"

The Man was silent. He marveled at the brilliance of the Glory. He marveled at the Love. It was not just the Woman's love. It was God's Love. It was God's Grace. The Man smiled. It was so simple!

"So simple. Easy. **You just have to open your heart!**" he exclaimed. "I feel it. I don't understand, but I feel it! It is the Spirit!"

"I must go," she said. "I love you. Jehovah God loves you."

"Yes," he said. "I love you. I love Jehovah...and I will tell him so."

The Man rose. He waved the minister silent. The Man turned. He then spoke in a strong voice so that all who were gathered around could hear, "Please pray with me to God our Father, and to His Son...."

"George 6234."

"Yes, Lord?"

"Stay with the Man."

Finis

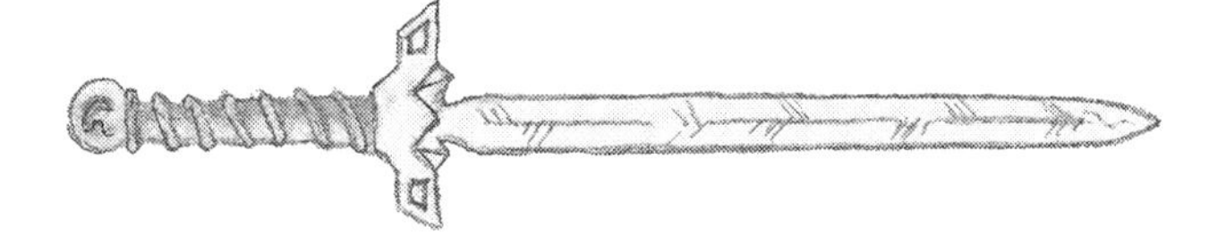

YOU JUST HAVE TO OPEN YOUR HEART

APPENDIX

Ahrim: younger demon and protégé of Ahriman.
Ahriman: older, very senior, experienced demon, and fallen angel.
Asmodeus: an older, senior demon and fallen angel.
Baba: older Eastern Europe witch, more powerful than most.
Demons: fallen angels.
Goblins: shock troops, usually controlled (if at all) by demons.
Loki: old world demon (but not fallen angel).
Loy, The Elder: an older demon, historian.
Lucifer: The Satan, The Dragon, the Tempter, Beelzebub, Baalzebul.
Moloch: an older demon and fallen angel.
Ogres: mean--not too smart, lowest on totem pole.
Temptation 16: a demon with a reputation.
Witches: lower level than demons.

¤

Cornelius: the Woman's guardian angel, a senior angel.
Cristobal: the Cousin's guardian angel.
Franciscus: the other pilot's guardian angel.
Gabriel: an archangel.
George 6234: a young, apprentice guardian angel.
Jehovah: God, YAHWEH, I AM.
Mercy 1021: the Friend's guardian angel.
Pliny: Agnes' Angel Legion acting Commander.
St. Agnes: monitoring Los Angeles; honored by having her own Angel Legion.

¤

The Man: the reason it happens.
The Woman: the Man's wife.
The Cousin: the Woman's cousin.
The Friend: the Woman's Friend.
The Farmhand: wrong place at the wrong time.

¤

A Glory, also a Gloria: radiance of light that may suddenly appear without apparent cause; also a ring, circle, nimbus, halo of light. These discs or flashes of brilliant light are considered by many to be the signs of God's Grace and protection.

Atheist: one who denies the existence of God.

Agnostic: one who believes it is impossible to know anything about God and refrains from commitment to any religious doctrine.

Gehenna: Hell.

Memphis: the place where it all happens (in the Texas Panhandle on US 287).

Sheol: place of utter destruction, total darkness and total silence.

Tartarus: home of the fallen angels.

ABOUT THE AUTHOR

A graduate of the United States Air Force Academy with an MPA from Auburn University, Jon Anthony Gallo, served on active duty in the Air Force for 26 years with assignments as a jet fighter pilot, International Politico-Military Affairs Officer and Base Commander. The recipient of aviation combat awards and the Legion of Merit, his assignments included the Philippine Islands, Thailand, Germany, and Italy. After retiring from the Air Force, Jon worked as a DC-10 Training Instructor, and then worked directing air shows, balloon festivals and air races. He also served as a faculty advisor and adjunct instructor for Embry Riddle Aeronautical University. Jon and his wife, Jacquie, live in Colorado and have three children, ten grandchildren, two great-grandchildren and two cats.

Made in the USA
Charleston, SC
16 June 2012